The Old Jest

Jennifer Johnston received exceptional critical praise for *The Old Jest*.

'Jennifer Johnston has excelled . . . Her portraits are subtle, drawn from the heart and we deeply care about each one.' *Spectator*

'A beautifully written, precise and touching portrait of an eighteen-year-old girl whose cosy childhood cocoon is about to be smashed by the violence outside.' *Sunday Express*

'Resonant, intelligent, evocative and moving – Jennifer Johnston at her best.' *Times Literary Supplement*

'Establishes her once again as one of Ireland's foremost writers.' *Irish Times*

'A delightful novel . . . marvellously light touch.' *Sunday Telegraph*

'Jennifer Johnston has established herself as the contemporary chronicler of the Anglo-Irish.' *The Listener*

'A beautifully composed novel.' *Sunday Times*

'A complex, painful truth made, not simple, but its complexity clear.' *Financial Times*

'It is like music to read – a melodious and lyrical novel.' *Country Life*

'Atmospheric memorable, intuitively poetic . . . her faultless writing. *The Old Jest* brings to the vicissitudes of violence an open-eyed, uncorrupted vision. *The Scotsman*

'There is the perfect adjustment of means to ends that one associates with Jane Austen . . . a novel of truth and charm, *The Old Jest* has the completeness, the detachment and something of the transparency of a floating bubble.' *London Review of Books*

Jennifer Johnston

The Old Jest

FLAMINGO

Published by Fontana Paperbacks

First published by
Hamish Hamilton Ltd 1979
First issued in Fontana Paperbacks 1980
Second impression November 1982

This Flamingo edition first published
in 1984 by Fontana Paperbacks,
8 Grafton Street, London W1X 3LA

Printed and bound in Great Britain by
Richard Clay (The Chaucer Press) Ltd,
Bungay, Suffolk

For D.S.T.G. with love

5 August 1920

Momentous day. The sun is shining. That in itself is not momentous – merely, for August, surprising.

The house sits sideways to the sea and facing south, so all the rooms are filled with sun. Judging by the haze on the horizon, almost like steam rising off the sea, the sun is shining everywhere, not just on this stretch of the east coast of Ireland, but in Cork, Skibbereen, Belfast, Galway and Kilkenny; drying up the grass and causing anxiety to the farmers. Weather seems permanently to be causing anxiety to the farmers. Even in England, where I have never been, the sun is shining. We read this in the newspaper which arrives in time for breakfast every morning and keeps Aunt Mary occupied for half an hour or so.

If you climb up the hill at the back of the house, you can see Wales on a clear day. It's not really very exciting, just a grey lump in the distance, but it's somewhere else. Somewhere new. For the last two weeks there has been no sign of Wales at all, just that pale haze steaming gently up into the sky, shutting this island off from the rest of the world.

The morning trains from Dublin have been filled with people coming down from the city to sit on the beach, and paddle and throw stones into the sea, and shout at their children, who change as the hours go by from pale city children to fretful whiners grilled beyond endurance by the unexpected sun. They stay mainly up at the far end of the beach, near to the station, and the two small cafés that sell fruit drinks and ice creams, and plates of biscuits and delicious cups of reviving tea. They don't in fact bother us over here at all. Two special trains have to be put on in the late afternoon to bring them back to town, as they don't all fit on the five-thirty from Wicklow. They leave an awful mess on the sand but the tide takes care of most of that. Poor Mr Carroll the stationmaster, however, has a terrible time keeping his station clean and tidy, and is the one person in the village to admit to being glad that heatwaves don't happen too often.

Momentous.

It is my eighteenth birthday.

I feel this to be a very important landmark in my life. I have left school. Yesterday I bundled away into the attic everything that had to do with school; the clothes, the books, the rules for living that for so many years they have tried to impose upon me; even the photograph albums, full of the snapshots of friends whom I have no impassioned desire to see again.

Today I want to start to become a person. My new year. My life is ahead of me, empty like the pages of this book, which I bought myself as a birthday present. It is not really a diary, more passing thoughts that give impressions of me, so that in forty years, if, as Bridie would say, I am spared, I can look back and see what I was like when I started out. It is so easy to forget. I have noticed that from watching Aunt Mary, not to mention Grandfather, but then he is a special case, being slowly devoured by extreme old age.

I suppose I shouldn't really have started off by mentioning the weather, only that maybe in forty years' time I will like to know that the sun was shining on the day I first began to look at the world.

There always seems to have been a war. I suppose in forty years things will be much the same, in spite of what people say to the contrary. Even in this small village so many people have been killed. There was my Uncle Gabriel who fell at Ypres, and has his name memorially written on the wall of the Church, with the Rector's son and Mrs Tyrell's brother, who, Aunt Mary said, was a rake and a philanderer, but nonetheless no one would have wanted him to be blown to smithereens by a bullet from a bearded

Turk. Father Fenelon's brother and Sammy Carroll from the station, and Paddy Hegarty, the fish man's son, who lost the sight of his right eye and is now a little gone in the head. There are more from round and about only I can't think of them all at the moment. Then Phil Ryan was killed when the British shelled Sackville Street, and Barney Carney was shot last week coming out of a dance hall in Bray, by the Black and Tans. They said it was a mistake. Perhaps they're all better off where they are; that's what Bridie suggests anyhow; whether it's Heaven or Hell, it can't be any worse than it is here. I don't think I agree with her. In spite of the terrible things that happen, I feel it is a great privilege to be alive.

Aunt Mary gave me a tennis racket for my birthday. She hopes in her heart that I will be a good sport and a social success, but I think she is prepared for disappointment. Bridie has made me a cake, which I'm not supposed to know about. Grandfather is beyond giving presents to people. I got seven cards from old school friends and a box of chocolates from Jimmy the gardener, which is really very very kind of him as he doesn't have money to throw around. I can hear him now below my window slowly moving the rake over the gravel. He seems to be impervious to either heat or cold, always moving at his own speed, tying, raking, weeding, sowing, his hands now like ancient roots themselves, searching their way back to peace in the soft earth.

I have no parents. This makes other people either sad or slightly embarrassed from time to time, but as I have never had any, I am used to the situation by now. Aunt Mary is both mother and father to me, a really very satisfactory state of affairs.

There are traces of my mother everywhere: photographs in delightful silver frames, in albums, or tucked into the frames of looking glasses which are now beginning to spot with age and the dampness of the winters. Like Aunt Mary she always seems to be smiling, and her hair curls in charming question marks over her high forehead. On my dressing table, which was once hers, as everything in my room was once hers, is a silver hairbrush with her entwined initials on the back. There are also handkerchiefs in one of

11

the top drawers that I have never been able to bring myself to use. I sleep in the same bed that she slept in as a girl. The same branches tap against the window in the winter storms. The same boards creak under my feet as I climb the bending stairs up to this room, our room at the top of the house. She gave me life eighteen years ago and I killed her. There's gratitude for you.

There has never been any trace of my father in my life. No one ever mentions his name or tells funny stories about him. No face in the dusty albums is ever pointed out as his. Do I owe my slightly beaky nose to him? My straight fine hair? Were his second toes, like mine, slightly longer than his big toes? Is he alive or dead? Good or bad? Sad or gay? No one seems to care. Since the age of about ten I have looked for him. I have stared at middle-ageing men as they passed me in the street, or sat opposite to me in the train on the way up to school in the morning. I have studied hands, hair, ears, skin textures in trams, trains and other people's houses. Though by now good sense has taken over from curiosity, I find I still have the disconcerting habit of staring at strange men, a habit I am trying to break myself of. I am curious to know what sort of a man he could have been to have disappeared as irrevocably as he did.

At least I know where she is. Under a neat rectangle of grass in the small Church of Ireland graveyard on the side of the hill above the village. The hill slopes down towards the sea and the Church crouches for shelter among the dark yew trees, bruised constantly by the winter wind, which blows relentlessly off the cold sea. The churchyard wall is low enough for those ghosts, nostalgic for the world, to see the roofs of the village tumbling down towards the sea, without having to disturb themselves in any way.

My uncle Gabriel is there, too, beside my mother, or rather some of him is there, as, according to Aunt Mary, they didn't find much of him to bury; but Grandfather insisted on his re-interment after the war was over. It was a sad occasion. Bridie said at the time that if anyone had asked her advice, she'd have said to leave the poor man where he was, no good ever came out of shifting bones around the place, and she cried a lot. My grandmother is up there, too, waiting, I imagine, somewhat impatiently for Grandfather to join her. There are upstanding crosses and leaning ones, some moss-covered with the inscriptions almost unreadable. There are slabs on the ground and gravel-filled boxes. There are quite a few grassy hummocks with no names or remembering words attached, but Aunt Mary knows who lies in each grave and all about them, even back to the earliest Charles Dwyer Esq., 1698, late of the County of Cork. They all stare across the roofs at the sea, and on a clear day, if they're interested, they can see Wales.

'Nancy.'

Aunt Mary came out of her room on the floor below and closed the door quietly behind her. She crossed the landing and paused at the attic stairs.

'Nancy.'

She moved on and stopped for a moment again by the long glass at the top of the stairs. She patted her hair. A large bun at the nape of her neck counterbalanced the slightly forward droop of her head.

'Darling . . . it's time. It's time.'

'Coming.'

Nancy came out of her room and ran down the stairs after her aunt.

'The house will fall down one day,' said Aunt Mary plaintively as Nancy landed with a thud beside her in the hall.

'Tra la.'

'I met Harry in the village and persuaded him back for luncheon. After all . . . he seemed delighted.'

The sun dazzled them both as they went out of the hall, and they stood blinking for a moment until their eyes had recovered from the shock.

'He's in the kitchen breaking the news to Bridie.'

'Oh,' was all that Nancy could bring herself to say.

Dear, dear Harry!

Clumps of lavender made the air smell sweet. She pulled a few leaves off and crumpled them with her fingers.

Harry.

As they turned the corner of the house, the old man's

mumbling voice crept towards them. 'Must not forget.' It was like an old gate creaking in the wind. 'Not forget.'

He sat in his wheelchair under a large black and white umbrella, which kept the sun out of his eyes and off the top of his head. His hands were clenched round a pair of field glasses, and, as he stopped speaking, he raised them and trailed them along the length of the railway line, which ran below them on the top of a bank between the distant fields and the sea. Nothing moved on the line or in the field; not even a tired bird disturbed the stillness of the air.

'Did you have a nice sleep, pet?'

Aunt Mary manoeuvred her way under the umbrella and kissed the top of his panama hat. He didn't appear to notice.

'Drinks,' she said, straightening up, her hand for a moment lingering on his shoulder. She turned and went in through the drawing-room window. Nancy sat down on the warm top step and leaned her back against the terrace wall.

'There won't be a train until half-past one, Grandfather. There's no point in looking now.'

He gave a little knowing laugh.

'I see other things than trains.'

'Mysteries, mysteries.'

She pulled a daisy out of a crack in the steps and began plucking at the petals. He loves me, he loves me not, he loves me . . .

'Remind me to tell her.'

'Silly.'

Loves me not, loves . . .

The old man's arms must have become tired, they drooped with the glasses down towards the plaid rug that even on the warmest day held his cold bones together. His eyes drooped too and his head sighed slowly forward. His breath crackled.

. . . loves . . . loves me, I know, loves me not.

A bee droned in the lavender and the sound of a piano climbed slowly up the hill towards them. Chopin.

Nancy threw the mutilated daisy down on to the step beside her.

Chopin. A shaky start and then the white fingers asserted their power and the music became rhythmic, confident. Nancy scowled at a passing butterfly.

'The darkness deepens, Lord with me abide,' sang the old man in his sleep, inspired no doubt by the music.

Nancy saw the straight figure of Maeve, her back to the window, the sun on her strong fingers as they squeezed the music from the keys. Her half-shadowed face had the pale and polished look of the nuns who pass you in the city streets.

Laughter and the clink of glasses. For a moment there was a hesitation in the music but by the time Aunt Mary and Harry came out of the house confidence was established once more.

Harry held a bottle of champagne in one hand and struggled with the cork.

'I gather it's a celebration. Wasn't I lucky to meet Mary in the village?'

Aunt Mary had a bunch of glasses slotted between her fingers.

'We have very few bottles left. It's pre-war. After all, you're not eighteen every day. I love champagne. Love it. Put a cushion under your behind, dear, or you'll get piles.'

'No one,' said Nancy, 'could get piles sitting on this. It's boiling. Positively burning.'

'Do what you're told.'

Nancy got up to collect a cushion from a deckchair.

Pop.

'Hurrah!'

Aunt Mary rushed a glass under the bubbles.

'Ooops! Bridie, come on out. Champagne. Darling Father, wake up. Hold it tight, pet.' She pushed a glass into his surprised hand. He opened his eyes.

'Ah, how joyful!' he whispered.

'It's Nancy's birthday. A joyful day.'

Bridie appeared around the corner, wrapped in her enormous, startlingly white apron. Harry gave her a glass and for a moment they all stood, arms outstretched, looking at Nancy. Bridie spoke first.

'God is good.' She knocked back the drink in one fell swoop. Everyone laughed.

'Happy birthday, Nancy.' Harry advanced towards her. She bent her head and saw his shining shoes moving with purpose in her direction. 'I shall kiss you.'

She turned her face away so that the kiss landed like a falling petal on her hot cheek.

'Gosh!' he said, 'you're boiling. Whatever have you been doing?'

She blushed even more and dipped her head down towards her glass. The bubbles rushed up her nose and she sneezed.

'I'll give yez ten minutes and then it's lunch,' announced Bridie. She marched away, helping herself to some more wine from the bottle as she passed it.

'Whose birthday?' asked the old man.

'That's Maeve playing, isn't it?'

Harry stood close beside her as he asked the question, the sleeve of his cream silk shirt touching her bare arm.

She nodded.

'Marvellous.'

'Nancy's birthday, darling. She's eighteen. Nancy!'

'Nancy!' He took a sip from the glass in his hand. 'My mother's name was Nancy.'

'Yes, pet, that's why we called Nancy, Nancy.'

'Marvellous.'

Just the music dancing. No breath of breeze to blow the sound away.

'Where is death's sting?' said the old man suddenly.

'Oh Father, really! Be well, be well today.'

He put the glass down on the table beside him and lifted the field glasses to his eyes. On the railway a lone engine and tender puffed its way along the line.

'That is interesting.' His voice was clear, momentarily almost young.

'What is?'

He let the glasses fall on to his knees and turned to her.

'There was something I had to tell you.'

'Yes, pet?'

She wandered over to the bottle and picked it up.

'Champagne doesn't go very far.'

She shared out the remains into everyone's glasses.

'I saw Robert on the line this morning.'

The music had stopped and his words seemed very loud.

16

'Who is Robert?' asked Harry, slightly interested.

Aunt Mary moved abruptly to the top of the steps.

'No, Father.' Her voice was exasperated.

'Or maybe it was yesterday.'

She moved down the steps, the drink in her hand swirling and bubbling with each step she took.

'There is no Robert.'

'But I tell you. I tell you.'

He raised a feeble hand and pointed towards the line.

Aunt Mary paid no heed to him. With quick movements of her finger and thumb she was snapping the dead heads off the roses as if it were the only thing in the world that mattered.

'Who is Robert?' Harry sat down beside Nancy on the step, regardless of piles. She didn't answer. She clasped her hands tight round the cold bowl of her glass. Sparks of light covorted on the distant sea.

'Nancy?'

She shook her head.

'I don't know!'

Robert Gulliver had been her father's name.

'He's potty,' she muttered.

'Oh come on Nancy . . .'

'He's always seeing things. It gets awfully boring. And singing hymns and . . .'

'He's old.'

Aunt Mary came towards them across the grass. In the summer she always wore a large straw hat to protect her tender northern skin from the sun. When she became either hot or fussed, little pears of sweat clung to the side of her nose like dew. She waved her empty glass gaily at them as if she'd been away for a very long time.

'Happy day . . .'

'Hold Thou Thy cross before my closing eyes . . .'

'There are so many jolly hymns and he has to choose the gloomy ones. Always the gloomy ones.'

'He's old.'

Aunt Mary panted slightly as she came up the steps. Soon, thought Nancy, she would start to become old, tremble as she picked up her knife and fork, falter on the stairs, fidget.

She moved slowly across the terrace and put her glass on the table, then she touched the old man's shoulder. Her hand, like her face, was pale and there were deep shadowy clefts between the bones.

'Robert is dead,' she said.

They both remained quite still, remembering, and then with an abrupt gesture she took off her hat and dropped it on the table beside the glass. At this moment Maeve began to play again. A mazurka, almost strident.

'Ah!' sighed Harry.

'If yez want your food hot, yez had better come in and get it,' Bridie's voice called out through the window.

She lacks a certain old world elegance, thought Nancy, getting up from her cushion.

Harry stretched his hand out towards Aunt Mary.

'Madame . . .'

She took it with a little bow.

'One and two and three and . . .'

They danced along the terrace.

'Damn!' said Nancy under her breath.

She took hold of the old man's chair and pushed him after the dancers.

From the village to the point the beach stretched for about two miles. It was a narrow strip of grey stones and coarse sand which shelved fairly steeply into the sea. The movement of the waves threw a million pebbles inwards and then pulled them away again from the land, eternally grinding, polishing, sucking and spewing. There was never silence, even on the calmest day. The railway line rose severely behind the beach, protecting the fields from the frequently angry sea, decorated only by the singing poles that carried the telegraph wires down the coast. Below the line, at the back of the beach, piles of huge granite blocks were tumbled in what seemed to be a haphazard fashion. In the winter the sea pounded against them, sending fountains of spray high into the air, and in the summer they sparkled like diamonds when the sun shone. If you managed to reach the point, you could see as far as your eyes would let you the curves of sand and rock, and the poles, and the charming

18

low hills, which graduated in the distance to blue mountains. No one ever walked as far as the point, though; it was not a very rewarding walk unless you enjoyed solitude and the company of the great white birds, who sat like ancient kings on the granite blocks staring inimicably into space. About halfway between the village and the point there was a solitary black bathing box, which had been put there by the convent for the convenience and privacy of the few nuns who liked to bathe. On summer days there were sometimes three or four of them there, looking like strange sea birds in their habits, their heads bent over their books, or towards each other in conversation. Nancy had seen them running in their long robes, laughing, or giving little breathless calls, into the sea. She would have liked to stop and watch them at times, but was afraid that her curiosity might offend them.

The hut was about half a mile beyond the point. It must have been built by some railway workers many years before, and was cleverly hidden in among the granite blocks, which protected it from the sea wind. It was a rectangular wooden hut with a sloping roof. The day she had found it had been a wild spring day. The waves tore at the shore and the wind sang gloriously in the telegraph wires. She had spent the best part of two hours scraping away the sand with her hands before the door would open enough to let her peer in. Then she knew that for all those years the hut had been waiting for her. She pushed the door shut again and climbed up on to the line. She walked along the sleepers until she came to the spot that she had always considered to be almost in range of Grandfather and his glasses, then she slithered down the grassy bank into the field and went up through the trees towards the house. Now she had a secret. She had always found it very difficult to keep secrets. She would have to be careful.

Over the next few weeks she had appropriated from around the place an old sweeping brush, worn down very low on one side, a hammer and nails, a couple of almost threadbare blankets, and two cushions out of which long white feathers constantly pricked their way. She had scrubbed at the floor with sea water until the planks had become the colour of old bones. She had hammered up shelves on which she kept a selection of books, an excellent tin with some ginger biscuits for eating after bathing, and a glass sweet jar filled with curious shells and stones that she had collected from time to time on the beach. She had moved the sand from round the door, oiled the rusted hinges, and screwed a hook into the cross beam inside on which to hang her towel. She had wondered about painting the walls, but decided against it. Gentility was not her aim.

No one seemed to notice the fact that she wasn't hovering uneasily around the house as she had always done before during school holidays. Aunt Mary was always preoccupied with her own routines: her chores routine, her reading routine, her golf routine, bridge, friends, racing routines, minding Grandfather and worrying inside herself. Not much time left in her day for wondering what Nancy was up to.

Nancy knew what would happen as soon as lunch was over; birthday or no birthday, Aunt Mary would drift away from the dining room and shut herself away in the study. It was her reading time, and, after she had read and digested for an hour, it would be gardening time. She would trim and clip and weed, tie back the climbing roses and the clematis, prune and snip in the greenhouse, collect dead heads into a large chip basket, and remove any snails she might come across from the flowerbeds and leave them in rows on the gravel for someone less squeamish than herself to exterminate. The old man, back once more by the drawing-room window, would let his head loll on to his chest and snores would bubble gently from his throat. Harry would fidget and chat and wonder in his head what excuse he could make to go and visit Maeve.

Nancy slipped out of the room while they were sitting round the table stirring their coffee lethargically with tiny silver spoons.

As she crossed the avenue and skirted the little wood below the house, a warm breeze sighed through the trees. For the first time for weeks the leaves stirred, almost imperceptibly, like sleepers about to wake. The movement came from the south-west. Soon the weather would change – perhaps not today, but soon. She could smell the sea as she crossed the field. A gull drifted gently above her, fully stretched on the lifting wind. She took off her shoes and scrambled up the bank on to the rails. Under her bare feet the sleepers were warm and ridged, comfortable.

'Robert is dead.'

Aunt Mary's voice had been neither sad nor glad when she had spoken the words. Matter of fact. We will have no more of this nonsense. Robert is dead, no carry on, father dear. Who? Whom then had he seen? Who had moved him to remember?

No one. Probably some figure in his mind, out of the mist of the past. Peering through time. Anyway he was potty. If one had to choose a name for a father, one wouldn't choose Robert. Oh no. Something a little more exotic perhaps. Constantine or Artemis, or heroic, like Alexander. Why should he be dead? I don't see it like that.

She bathed when she reached the hut. The coarse sand was burning hot and her feet arched with shock as she ran to the edge of the sea. The sea itself, in spite of this, was almost ice cold. There were no concessions made here to the dabbler or paddler; the beach shelved steeply and within a few yards of the shore you were out of your depth and being tugged gently down the coast, heading, unless you were careful, for some unknown destination. She lay on her towel afterwards to dry in the sun, and stared at the clouds that were now beginning to build up round the rim of the horizon. It must have been almost four when she remembered Bridie's cake. She stood up and began to brush the sand from her shoulders and the backs of her legs. Suddenly she felt as if she were being watched,

'Hello.'

No one was on the line or the beach. No one moved. A drop of rain burst on her cheek.

'Damn!' She glared up at the sky, innocent and empty above her. The sand stirred cautiously. She moved up to the hut. At the door she paused for a moment and looked round again.

'Hello.'

She went in and dressed. Several more drops landed on the roof.

She shook the towel out of the door.

'Hellooo . . . ooo.'

A gull on one of the granite blocks looked sideways at her with one of its mean eyes.

'Why shouldn't there be someone here?' she asked it reasonably. 'After all, it's supposed to be a free country, and don't stare at me like that.'

The bird turned its back on her, its claws clamping impatiently on the stone. It looked too relaxed for there to be lurkers around. She hung the towel on the back of the door. Rain was now scattering itself on the roof and sand. She shut the door carefully so that the rain couldn't blow in and rot the floor, then she climbed up on to the track and ran most of the way home.

They were in the drawing-room just about finishing their tea when she arrived.

Harry was still there. He had always been a glutton for cucumber sandwiches and pale China tea, and Maeve, she thought with resignation.

'I'm still here,' he said somewhat unnecessarily.

'Have some tea,' said Aunt Mary. 'It'll be cold though.'

'No thanks.'

'We haven't cut the cake yet. It's been a sore temptation, though.'

'Where did you disappear off to?' His voice was slightly plaintive.

'She's always disappearing. She leads a secret life. I'm terribly good, I never ask. Do I, darling?'

'No sandwiches left?'

'You can't expect . . .'

'Quite.'

'Let's all have some cake. You cut it, darling. The birthday girl must cut the cake.'

'And wish,' said Harry.

Nancy picked up the knife and sank it through the chocolate icing. I wish . . . wish that he won't say how about us popping down to see Maeve. The first slice.

'It looks marvellous. A real Bridie special. You are lucky to have her, Mary.'

'Cake, Grandfather?'

22

'Cake,' he repeated uneasily, leaving no one the wiser.

She cut a small piece and put it on a plate. She carried it over to him and put it down on the small round table beside him.

'It's my birthday. Remember? Eighteen.'

He peered up at her face for a moment, struggling in his mind to place her.

'Ah!' he said finally. 'Yes. Helen's girl . . .' There was a flash of triumph in his eyes.

'Never eat cake.'

Nonetheless she left the plate beside him, in case he changed his mind.

'You're wet,' said Aunt Mary.

'Only a bit. The rain came down so suddenly.'

'I should go and change if I were you.'

'Not on my birthday,' said Nancy firmly.

'Rheumatism . . .'

'Nobody of eighteen gets rheumatism.'

'My dear child, you have to take care . . .'

'I . . . er . . . thought . . .' Harry spoke through a mouthful of cake '. . . thought that we might pop down and see Maeve. Just for a few secs.'

Nancy walked over to the window and looked out at the sparkling rain. So much for wishes. He was so blooming predictable. She could never work out why she had such . . . well . . . tender feelings for him. Loving, tender feelings. Perhaps because of his predictability. There were no dangerous possibilities to be beware of in his personality. He might bore you to death? Not if you loved him.

'It's a monkey's wedding,' she said.

'I beg your pardon?'

Aunt Mary was collecting tea cups and saucers on to the tray.

'She means it's raining while the sun is shining.'

'Good heavens! I wonder why?'

'Why what?'

'Why it's called a monkey's wedding.'

'Why not?' Nancy asked.

'It's a pity you missed the cucumber sandwiches. Bridie makes superb cucumber sandwiches, Mary.'

'You have to cut the bread really thin. That's the secret. No point in having them if the bread isn't thin. And the pepper of course. It has to be just right.'

She removed the untouched plate of cake from beside the old man.

'If you'll excuse me, I'll just bring the tray out to the kitchen. Bridie likes to get down to the Church early on Saturday.'

As she left the room he went over to Nancy.

'How about it?'

'All right. If you want to.'

'Just pop down.'

'Now?'

'Yes . . . ah . . . yes . . . Why not?'

'It's raining.'

'Monkey's . . .'

'Yes.'

'You're wet already.'

She sighed.

'Let's go then.'

As they stepped out through the long window on to the terrace, the old man's voice followed them.

'Swift to its close ebbs out life's little day, Earth's joys grow dim, its glories pass away : Change and decay . . .'

'We're off, Aunt Mary, goodbyeee. Off to see Maeve. Popping down . . .' She began to laugh.

'Change. Change, dear child, out of your wet . . . Change '

Nancy hustled Harry down the steps.

'Hurry Harry. Harry hurry. Hurry hurry.'

'Nancy . . .'

'Oh hush, Harry! Don't fuss like her. After all, if I go back and change my clothes, Maeve may have gone out. Or anything. Snatch the day . . . didn't someone say that? In Latin or something?'

'Why does he sing like that all the time? I mean all the time you were out he sang and sang. He didn't seem to notice he was doing it. That hymn is so gloomy too.'

'Oh, I don't know. "I triumph still if Thou abide with me." Anyway it'll probably be something else tomorrow. You know the way sometimes a song seems to fill your

24

mind. No matter what you do you can't get rid of it. It just
goes on and on in your head. He's very keen on Tom Moore.
"Oft in the Stilly Night." Rather sombre ones like that.
Considering how potty he is, he's marvellous at remembering the words.'

Daringly she took his arm. He didn't resist. He was always
very polite like that.

'Can I ask you something.'

'Go ahead.'

'You don't have to answer if you don't want to.'

'Do come to the point.'

'Did you enjoy being in the war?'

He stopped walking and stood looking at a yellow rose
which was about to unfold itself at the end of a stiff green
stem.

'What an odd thing to want to know.'

A slight frown worried his forehead.

'I'm curious. I ask curious questions.'

He bent a little towards the flower. She felt the rose's life
would be over and done with before he answered the question.

'Enjoy . . . that's an odd word, Nancy . . .'

She waited.

'Well, I suppose I must admit to enjoying moments here
and there. Here and . . . I suppose I didn't mind it. Let's put
it like that. What's the name of that rose?'

'Were you afraid?'

'I didn't really notice.'

'Afraid of killing someone?'

'Silly child. A lot of use that would have been.'

'Of being killed than?'

She clicked her fingers in a final gesture.

'Not much point really. Oh, from time to time you got
a sort of guzzy in your guts. Not a prolonged feeling of
fear, though. I can't think why you want to know. Tired.
I think that's what I remember feeling most. You learnt to
control fear so well that you almost forgot about it. The
rose?' he reminded her.

'I haven't the foggiest idea. You'll have to ask Aunt
Mary. She knows the names of all the flowers and trees . . .

in the world probably. Birds too. Did you feel like a hero?'

'Of course not.' He laughed. 'There were some heroes all right, but not me. After all, I come from a long line of soldiers, not heroes. Just straightforward soldiers. Good at their job. It didn't appeal to me as a job, though. I suppose times have changed a bit. I think the parents were disappointed when I got out. Especially Mother. She always saw me as a budding general. You know mothers.'

'No,' said Nancy.

He blushed.

'Oh Lord, Nancy! I am sorry. What a ghastly thing to say! It just sort of slipped out.'

She nudged him into walking on. The grass was slippery under their feet. It needed cutting. It seemed to have grown in the unexpected rain.

'Well . . .'

'Well?'

'How about being a stockbroker . . . does that appeal to you as a job?'

'You're so immature.'

'Hey . . .' Her voice was indignant.

'What I mean is . . . when you're older you won't bother people with such stupid questions.'

'But I want to know. How do you find things out if you don't ask questions?'

He sighed for her.

'It seems to me nobody ever tells you anything, talks to you. I have a lot of time to make up. My head is full of questions. Have you a burning desire to be a stockbroker?'

'You have to do something. You'll find that out one day. Rather, men have to do something. Build a career, earn money, accept responsibility. You know perfectly well what I mean. Stockbroking is as good a way of making money as any other. Anyway it's good to be a girl . . . none of those bothers. You just wait until some bloke comes along and lays it all at your feet.'

She didn't reply. They walked in silence towards the gate in the high hedge that separated the Caseys' garden from the field.

'Burning desire.' His voice was reflective rather than con-

26

temptuous. 'I suppose you're filled with burning desire?'

'Well . . . at this moment only to understand.' She laughed. 'Now you'll say I'm immature again. I can see it in your face.'

'What do you want to understand?'

He was getting a little bored with the conversation. His feet marched quicker towards the gate and Maeve and maturity.

'Everything . . . I suppose.' She gestured expansively with her hands.

He took a silver cigarette case from his pocket and helped himself to a cigarette. He tapped the end of it several times on the case before putting it in his mouth.

'It's all written down somewhere. When you get to college, you can busy yourself looking it all up.' Patronising, indulgent. He took out a box of matches and lit the cigarette.

'It's what isn't written down that worries me.'

'You could become a terrible bore. A crank.' Blue smoke escaped through his nose. She thought it looked terrific. They reached the gate. It was set deep in a hedge of escallonia, which rose high above their heads and smelled sweet after the rain. She stopped, her hand on the latch.

'I'd like to be safe. Things have always been so safe, protected. I feel . . .' Her fingers unconsciously rattled the latch. '. . . if you know things, it must help . . . you know when you have to move alone. Know and understand. You have to find out . . .' She looked at him. Smoke trailed from his lips. His head was slightly stooped to avoid the poking twigs above them. He peered past her, forwards into the light of the garden beyond.

'Oh well . . .' she said with resignation. She poked him with a finger.

'Hey . . . You. Do you think I'm pretty?'

'Oh . . . Nancy . . . I was thinking . . . away.' He looked her up and down. 'Not too bad. You'll improve. You're perhaps just a bit . . .'

'Immature?'

'That's the sort of thing. You know what I mean . . .'

She kicked the gate open with her right foot and they went into the Caseys' garden. Geometric beds were filled

27

with the tidiest of flowers. Even after the rain no petals had dared to drift on to the grass. The brick paths were weedless. The house had been built around the turn of the century of good red bricks. Bow windows opened on to the grass. A stone dolphin spouted water mysteriously from its tail into a pond. The sound of splashing water was agreeable, and the heavy evening scent of flowers.

'Ah!' said Harry. He liked order. 'Ahhhh!'

Nancy didn't say anything.

'I sometimes get the feeling,' he said with severity, 'that you don't like Maeve.'

'Oh, I do. I do.'

Harry looked at his half-smoked cigarette and wondered what to do with it. There was no place in this garden for litter. Carefully he pinched the glowing end between his fingers and pushed the debris into his pocket. Nancy watched every thought, every move. She could be malicious, he thought, a malicious prying child. She'd grow out of it. He made sure with his fingers that the cigarette was out before he took his hand out of his pocket.

'Does Maeve not smoke?'

'Of course not.'

'Aunt Mary does. There's nothing wrong with smoking.'

'Some people find it a disagreeable habit.'

'Coooeee!'

Maeve came out of a window to greet them.

'It's great to see you. I'm all alone. Mummy and Daddy have gone to a dinner or something up in town. I'm all alone. I hoped you'd drop in.' Her smile embraced them both, but her eyes remained on Harry's face. 'Harry,' she breathed.

'Well . . . ah . . . yes . . . ah . . . isn't it lucky we came. Isn't it, Nancy?'

'Oh, Nancy.'

'Hello,' said Nancy.

Maeve and Harry smiled at each other. They didn't notice the long silence that surrounded their smiling faces, pushing them closer and closer together. An angry pulse knocked inside Nancy's forehead. The flowers stretched complacently in the raked damp earth. No snails here to munch the

28

leaves, leave silver trails along the paths. Nancy looked with irritation at her right big toe, which was pushing its way untidily through the toe of her shoe.

'My blooming feet are still growing.' she said aloud. The smiling stopped.

'Pardon?' asked Maeve.

'Oh, nothing really . . . just my huge ever-growing feet . . . nothing interesting . . . nothing . . .'

'It's her birthday,' explained Harry. 'She's eighteen.'

'How gorgeous!' said Maeve, transferring the smile to Nancy. 'You don't look eighteen. Does she, Harry? I'd have got you a present if I'd known.' She leant forward and dropped a scented kiss on to Nancy's cheek. 'Gorgeous! No more school. Next thing she'll be getting married. Won't she, Harry? Come in. It's cold after the rain. I'll get you a present next week. Better late than never, that's a promise. What did you give her, Harry?'

She led them through the French windows into the drawing-room. It was an extension of the garden. Wherever you looked, flowers seemed to be climbing, twisting, bursting, in ordered profusion. Only the white concert grand piano, drawn across one corner of the room, was free from them.

'Well, actually, nothing yet. I didn't really know in time. Forgot. I'm hopeless about that sort of thing. Hopeless. What would you like, Nancy?'

'Yes, Nancy, what would you like?'

'I don't really . . .'

'I insist,' said Harry. 'Absolutely insist.'

'There must be something . . .' said Maeve.

Nancy considered the matter.

'Anything?'

'Within reason of course.'

'Of course,' agreed Nancy.

'Nancy would never take advantage,' said Maeve.

Maeve and Harry smiled at each other again as Nancy considered.

'I'd like to go to the Abbey. Would you take me to the Abbey?'

'By all means.'

'What a gorgeous idea! May I come too? Please may I come?'

'Of course,' said Harry, charmed with the idea.

'You wouldn't mind, would you, Nancy?'

'Why should I mind?' Nancy bared her teeth at them both.

'Well now, isn't that lovely? Harry will arrange it all and we'll all have a lovely evening. Gorgeous.'

'Gorgeous,' said Nancy.

'So we'll celebrate now with a glass of sherry. You could have whisky, Harry, if you prefer, but Nancy and I will . . .'

She moved towards the door.

'I'll give you a hand.'

'Really no need.' But she smiled into his face and they left the room together.

Nancy sat down with a thump on the blossoming sofa.

Why did I come?

Because he wanted to come. He was visibly dying to come. He wouldn't have had the gumption to come on his own.

They don't want me here.

No. Only needed your presence to get them through the first smile.

Now. Are they touching hands in the other room? Palm to palm is holy palmer's kiss.

Why do I prefer the inimical seagulls to the amiable girl?

Why does he . . . ?

Laughter from the next room.

Prefer . . .

Palm to palm.

Her.

The clink of glasses almost touching.

To . . . to . . .

The room smelled of floor polish and sweet drooping roses.

I find myself a pain in the neck.

She stood up.

'I must go home now.' She inclined her head graciously towards the piano. 'It has been delightful . . . thank you . . .'

She moved slowly towards the door, nodding, smiling at the chairs, the bowls of flowers, the table on which stood or rather pirouetted a bedizened shepherdess. 'So nice. . . so kind, au revoir . . .'

Once in the garden, she ran down the path and out through the gate in the hedge.

The gate squealed as she closed it behind her.

'Traitor,' she whispered.

Up the hill smoke drifted from two chimneys, staining the sky: one would be the range in the kitchen, where Bridie would be creaking and humming as she cooked the dinner; the other the newly lighted drawing-room fire, the flames crackling through the structure of sticks and turf.

As she walked across the field, the anger died inside her.

'Happy birthday me,' she said aloud.

8 August

It has been raining solidly since my birthday, but today the weather seems to be clearing. There are pale streaks of blue in the sky and from time to time sunlight enlivens the flowerbeds for a few moments. The swallows who spend so much of their time rattling around in the eaves just over the head of my bed are swooping and flitting outside the window. They move so fast. A flash of feathers and they are gone, and then moments later breathlessly back again. They are such excited birds. To be alive seems to give them so much pleasure.

Grandfather has been poorly for the last two days. He has twice fallen out of his chair. He never hurts himself when this happens, as he seems to fall in a completely relaxed and unstruggling way. He then lies helplessly on the floor, and Aunt Mary and I have great trouble in getting him back into his chair. Personally, I think he does it on purpose when he gets bored with his dreaming and singing and scanning the railway line. Aunt Mary just says 'Tut!' crossly when I suggest this to her, but I know, I really know, by the look in his eye, that he is getting at us in some way. If he is left safely in bed when he is having one of these little attacks, he cries and moans all day as if he were being tortured. He also refuses to feed himself, and Aunt Mary has to waste her time sitting by his side pushing food into his mouth as a mother does with a naughty child. I hate him when he is like this. He won't wear his teeth, and mucus drains out of the corners of his eyes, and I despise myself for the violence of the feelings I hold towards him. I could at times happily hold a pillow over his crumbling face. Aunt Mary's brusqueness is completely obliterated when she is with him. Her capacity for tenderness is amazing. That angers me too. I want him to die before we become damaged by his decay.

Today, however, the sun will shine again and I will go down the beach to my seagulls and listen to the sea crushing the stones.

The sun shone. Steam rose cheerfully up from the lawns, and the earth in the flowerbeds became warm again to the touch.

They were finishing lunch. The tall windows were open and the breeze moved the curtains. The old man's head drooped forward on his chest. A shaft of sun lay on his pale, almost lifeless hands. Aunt Mary carefully scraped the spoon for one final time around the bowl in her hand and leant towards him.

'That's the last little bit, pet. There. You've been so good . . . today so . . . Bridie will be pleased to see your empty plate. There, pet.'

She pushed the spoon through his unresisting lips. It had been his own special spoon as a child. His twisted initials, J.D., decorated the handle.

She put the bowl down on the table and patted his knee. He didn't respond in any way, just stared down at his hands on the rug. She got up and went to the window.

'Some people decay,' she said in a low voice. 'Some lucky people just drop dead, but others . . . well . . . others. That's the way it is for him. We have to take good care of him. Somewhere inside he knows.'

'Knows,' repeated Nancy with contempt.

'We have to take good care of him. Anyway, he'll be better tomorrow. I can tell.'

In the hall the telephone rang. One long jangling ring and then a pause. Nancy got up and went out to answer it. As she picked the receiver from its stand, the bell jangled again.

'Hello.'

It was Harry.

'Oh, hello.' She tried not to sound too pleased to hear his voice.

'Where did you go? It was fearfully rude of you to bolt like that. Honestly, Nancy.'

'I just went. Impelled? Compelled? Which word should I use?'

'You're such a bad child at times.'

'I thought you'd be better off without me ... so ... I went home.'

'Without a word.'

'There'd have been such a fiddledeedee. Anyway I felt like a lonely ant lurking among all those flowers.'

'Tut!'

'I'm sure you were better off without me. Admit it.'

'I stayed for supper.'

'There you are. That couldn't have happened if I'd been there.'

'She was alone . . .'

'Yes.'

There was a pause. Mrs Burke in the post office coughed impatiently as she listened to their silence.

'It was about the theatre I rang.'

'Oh yes.'

'How about tomorrow night? That suits Maeve. Would it suit you?'

'Yes.'

'Sure?'

'Oh yes. Thank you. Thank you.'

'Shouldn't you ask Mary?'

'That'll be all right.'

'Very well then. Can you come up in the train and meet me at the office? College Street. We'll have a quick bite to eat. I'll bring the motor up and I can drive you home. Tell Mary you'll be all right.'

'That's sounds lovely.'

'Six at the office. It's *Riders to the Sea*, by the way.'

'Yes, I know.'

'That all right?'

'Yes.'

'Well   .'

'Well . . .

Mrs Burke coughed again.

'See you tomorrow.'

'Yes.'

'Goodbye.'

'Goodbye.'

She put the receiver back on the stand and turned the handle to let Mrs Burke know that the call was over . . . as if she didn't know already. She stood in the darkness for a moment listening to the sound of his voice murmuring inside her head.

'Who?' called Aunt Mary from the dining room.

Nancy moved.

'Harry.'

Aunt Mary was polishing the old man's face with a table napkin.

'He's taking me to the Abbey tomorrow night.'

'That'll be nice.'

Riders to the Sea.'

'Do take care of the Black and Tans and . . . trouble . . .'

'And Maeve,' said Nancy.

'Pretty girl.' Aunt Mary dropped the crumpled napkin on to the table. 'Tiresome, I find.'

'It's a birthday present.'

'Just take care. I suppose he'll take care of you really. He's dropped off to sleep. I think I'll bring him into the drawing-room. He always likes that window.'

'I think I'm in love with Harry.'

Aunt Mary leant down and took the brake off the wheel-chair.

'What nonsense!'

A cloud moved across the sun and for a moment the room was dim.

.'It isn't nonsense to me.'

'Maybe not, dear. I expect you just have a crush on him. That happens, you know. It's not love, though. Love is damn big, pet, don't consider it yet awhile. Anyway, Harry wouldn't be the right sort of person for you.'

The cloud moved on and the sun made patterns of brilliance on the floor and wall. Nancy didn't say a word.

'I don't mean he isn't nice, pet. He really is ... he's just not amazing in any way.'

'He's beautiful. Amazingly beautiful.'

Aunt Mary grasped hold of the handles and began to push the chair across the room. 'Beauty,' she said, 'as you know, is only skin deep. There's a flat sort of beauty and a ... well ... something more interesting. He's flat. He should have stayed in the army, he'd have made a perfectly beautiful general. Much more beautiful than Father ever was.'

'That's your opinion ...'

'What are you going to do with yourself this afternoon, now that the weather's better?'

'I thought I'd go for a walk. Bathe perhaps.'

'You should have friends of your own age. Play tennis. I played a lot of tennis at your age.'

'You've always been a sporty sort of person.'

'Bring a woollie. There's a cold wind.'

As they moved out into the hall, the old man, disturbed by the movement, began to sing.

'I 'fear no foe with Thee at hand to bless ...'

'Isn't that marvellous,' said Aunt Mary. 'He's getting better. Maybe I'll be able to get to the races after all tomorrow.'

'Ills have no weight and tears no bitterness.'

Nancy went out into the porch, which was filled with the sweet, heavy scent of geraniums.

'Woollie,' called out her aunt.

Everything seemed the same as usual. Safe. Unpeopled. The tide was ebbing and small waves frilled at the water's edge. A seagull, immobile on the roof ridge, stared at the horizon. Among the pounded shells to the right of the door lay a cigarette butt. Nancy frowned at it for a moment before kicking sand over it with her bare toe. She opened the door and looked into the hut. There was no one there; but someone had been there. Someone had moved and breathed there. Someone had touched her belongings, threatened her secret. For a moment she was angry and then frightened. Above her the bird shifted its claws on the roof. She became calm again. She took down a notebook and pencil from the shelf and began to write a note.

'Dear sir, I would be grateful if you didn't come here again. This is a very private and personal property. Yours sincerely Nancy Gulliver.'

Carefully she tore the page out of the notebook and stood, tapping the pencil against her teeth, looking round for a suitable place to leave the message. Finally she propped it up against the books on the shelf facing the door, just where it would catch the eye of anyone coming in through the door. The thought of swimming didn't really appeal to her any more, so she closed the door very carefully, waved to the seagull and went home.

Harry telephoned again the next morning as they were having their breakfast.

'Nancy.'

'Oh, hello.'

He's going to cancel it, she thought. Don't let him cancel it.

'I'm just dashing off to work.'

'Yes.'

Aunt Mary rustled the *Irish Times* with irritation.

'I just thought I'd ring and find out if Mary was happy about you coming up.'

'I told you. It's all right.'

'Your toast will get cold,' called Aunt Mary.

'Good. She doesn't mind you coming up alone on the train.'

'No.' Fuss, fuss.

'Remember not to get a return. I'll be driving you both home.'

'Yes.'

'There is nothing more awful than cold toast. People should have the manners not to use that damn machine at meal times.'

'I'll put the motor near the theatre so we won't have far to walk.'

'Yes.'

'So Mary needn't worry.'

'I don't think she is.'

'Toast.'

'That's all right then. I'll see you at the office. We'll snatch a quick bite to eat.'

'Thank you.'

'Half past six should be time enough.'

'Half six.'

'Half six is three,' shouted Aunt Mary's furious voice. 'At least use the language as it should be used.'

'I'd better be off.'

'Yes.'

'Goodbye.'

'Goodbye. Thank you for ringing.'

'The Germans,' said Aunt Mary from behind the paper, as Nancy sat down again, 'say half four when they mean half past three. *Halb vier. Halb fünf* . . . half past four. It's confusing, but then they're foreign. Different constructions and things. Eat your cold toast.'

'I don't think I want any more.'

'Fiddledeedee! Anyway there's all that butter and marmalade on it.'

She went back to the paper and Nancy ate her toast. At last Aunt Mary folded the paper neatly and tucked it under her arm. She stood up and collected the letters scattered in front of her plate.

'The paper is so sickening to read these days. I do wish this killing would stop. Poor Gabriel!' She sighed and stood for a moment staring across the room at nothing. 'I'm so glad in a way he isn't here. He would have found it all so upsetting. I know I do. It's the poor people . . . He always wanted Home Rule, you know.'

'Who?'

'Your Uncle Gabriel. Father used to get so upset with him. So angry. There's nothing like the Empire, he used to say. Poor little pet! I'd better go and see how he is this morning. Half past, don't forget . . . It's not only incorrect to say the other, it's terribly common.'

'Dear Miss Gulliver, thank you for your note. I can assure you that I am a great respecter of privacy and I regret that I have in any way impinged on yours. I feel sure that if you were to understand the circumstances, you would forgive me. You look like someone who would forgive. I have watched you. I saw you looking disturbed and angry as you became almost aware of my presence one afternoon. I will endeavour not to disturb you again. I hope you find everything today as you would wish to; no more cigarette ends, no stale air. I must say I am happy at your choice of books. What a piece of luck to find mental as well as physical sanctuary! I thank you. I also respect your famous name. Like he who held it before you were even thought of, I would claim to be a class of travelling man.'

It was unsigned.

It was pinned to the door with a long gold cravat pin, like the one that Uncle Gabriel used to pin through his stock on hunting days. Carefully she stuck it in the front of her shirt. A joker, she thought. She opened the door and looked into the hut. There was no trace of him at all. A joker. She climbed up over the granite blocks on to the railway line. As far as her eyes could see the beach was empty. The only movement was from the splinters of sun on the surface of the sea. A couple of gulls lazed on the wind. Behind, through the woods and up towards the hills, sheep browsed among the whins. She balanced herself on the rail.

'All right. All right. Joke over. Come on out, wherever you are.'

Her voice flew away into the silence.

'Ssssh!' whispered the sea reprovingly.

'I want to meet you.'

She waited for a moment, swaying slightly to balance herself.

'Please.' Bridie would have wanted her to say please. She repeated the word for good measure. There was no reply.

She jumped from the rail and scrambled back down to the hut. She collected a book and a rug and lay down in the sun to read and wait.

'Miss Nancy Gulliver?'

She hadn't heard him coming. He had climbed silently down over the blocks and stood about ten feet behind her. His feet were bare and had the stringy look of the roots of some old tree that had worked their way up out of the ground. He stood quite still while she inspected him. He was a small man. His hair was thick and soft and fell down each side of his face, making a dark frame for his bony features and water-pale eyes.

'You don't look well,' she said, after a lot of staring.

'I'm all right.'

'Who are you?'

'The traveller.'

She shook her head, irritated.

'I know that. But, who?'

'Dear child, don't be cross. I'm just a passing stranger. As the greatest writer either of these islands has yet managed to produce said . . . What's in a name?'

'I'd just like to know what you are.'

'Are you being philosophical or merely inquisitive?'

She blushed and looked away from him. The gull on the roof above them looked incredibly bored; its head was sunk down into its body, its eyes like stones.

'Won't you sit down?'

It had an idiotic drawing-room ring about it which made him smile briefly.

'Thank you.'

He moved, still quite silently, across the sand and sat down beside her on the rug. They sat in silence looking at the sea. The horizon was a hard clear line in the distance.

'It'll rain again,' he said.

'Yes.'

'I'm afraid the summer is over.'

She scooped up a handful of sand and let it trickle slowly through her fingers.

'Are you a criminal? That's really all I want to know.'

'No. I hope you'll believe that.'

'I'll believe whatever you tell me.'

'That's not always wise.'

'I haven't much experience of people telling lies.'

The formality of her voice made him smile again.

'I can see that.'

She looked straight into his face, offended by the remark.

'What do you mean by that?'

'Only, dear child . . . young lady I should say . . . that you are young . . . very young I would guess . . . and I don't believe that there are many dark alleys, either of the city of Dublin or in other people's minds that you have ever even peeped into.' He sighed. 'I can never understand why the young so despise their youth. Their one great attribute. Oh God, for the ability to be able to see again with innocent eyes!'

'Why did you choose my hut?'

He laughed.

'I don't suppose you'll believe me, but it was my hut long before you were even born.'

'I certainly don't.'

'I thought you were going to believe everything I said.'

'Not tall stories.'

'It's no tall story. I used to know this place as a child.' He smiled slightly. 'Even younger than you.'

She looked at him with interest.

'You come from round here?'

'In a way. The original line was washed away, you know.'

'Oh!'

'It used to be down below where the blocks are now. They had to rebuild it further back and higher. That would have been about thirty years ago. Yes. I remember bits of the old line being washed away in a huge storm one winter. The whole shape of the coast seemed to be changed after thet. I remember the men working on the line, the incredible almost musical noise of their hammers on the metal rails. Wagnerian.' He laughed. 'Only I didn't know about Wagner then. I was neither prodigy nor prodigal. To tell the truth it must have been quite a bit longer than thirty years. More like forty.'

'I'm raging.'

'Oh dear, I'm sorry!'

'It's not your fault. I had just dreamed myself into thinking that it was only mine.'

'It's very much yours now. Everything has changed so much. Only that bird is the same. I'd know her anywhere. Kittiwake,' he called up at the gull.

'Now that really is a tall story.'

'Seagulls are well known for their longevity.'

'Rot!'

'Maybe she's the Hag of Beare . . . relocated.'

'I've always thought it must be a male. He seems to have so much time to spare.'

'No, no. An aged female. Long past child-rearing age, who just sits and grimly contemplates the mess that other seagulls are making of the world.'

Nancy sighed.

'Yes. Perhaps you're right.'

She picked up another handful of sand and stared at it. Warm, grey gold, little fragments of shell and sparkles of mica.

'I have to go,' she said at last, still staring at the sand.

'So soon? We've barely met.'

'I have to go into town. I'm going to the Abbey Theatre.'

'That's nice.'

'Well . . yes . . . in a way.'

'I suppose you're going with some lucky young man.'

She threw the sand away.

'Well, in a way . . . I mean, he's not my young man. I . . . well . . . I like him a lot, but . . . She's coming too . . .'

'It happens to us all you know.'

'I'm a bit young Aunt Mary says.'

'Perhaps.'

She smiled at him. For a moment her face was illuminated, rare. He felt a need to touch her, but sensibly kept his hands to himself.

'I wouldn't worry,' he said instead.

'Oh, I don't. I don't worry. I do silly other things.'

She stood up and wiped the sand from her hands on her skirt. 'There's no need for you to hide away any longer.'

'Thank you. I'd rather not, I must say.'

She held her hand out towards him.

'Goodbye.'

He shook it. Rough sand still stuck to the palm.

'Goodbye, Nancy.'

'Is there anything you want?'

'I'm quite good at fending for myself. Just discretion.'

'I don't blab.'

'I'm sure you don't.'

She flapped her hand awkwardly at him and scrambled

42

up on to the line. When she looked back to catch a last sight of him, he was sitting on the rug with his back to her, staring at the sea.

She loved the station. Had always loved it – the big yard where the engines shunted backwards and forwards, sighed and puffed, groaned uneasily from time to time and then at moments of elation crashed and clattered their couplings together like a hundred chain-rattling ghosts running amok; the signal box along at the end of the platform, where Martin the signalman, when in a good mood, had let her climb up the steep wooden steps and watch him pull at the handles, hear the bells ringing from along the line and see the great signals moving slowly into place, red, crash, down, green, creeeak, up. There was also the metal bridge over the single track from the up platform to the down platform, where, if you stood as the engine passed below you, the whole world disappeared for a moment in a cloud of grey smoke.

'Evening, Nancy.'

'Good evening, Mr Carroll.'

Always important with the gold braid on his cap and his green flag tucked under his arm, the station was his pride and joy, the buildings spick and span, no peeling woodwork or smeared glass, long neat flowerbeds always cheerful at the back of the down platform.

'Up to the smoke?'

'Yes.'

'You want to mind yourself. Mind yourself these bad times. Sad times,' he muttered. 'Sad times.'

He must be thinking of Sammy, Nancy thought to herself. She put her hand out and touched his navy serge sleeve.

'I'm going to the Abbey Theatre,' she said, hoping that the information might cheer him up a little.

'Isn't that nice now for you? Some nice young fella in the case I'll be bound. Ey?' He winked.

Nancy smiled.

'Of course.'

'Aren't you growing up fast. It seems like only yesterday you were down here pestering the life out of me to let you have a ride on the turntable and now there's other things on your mind. How's your aunt?'

'She's well, thank you.'

'And the giniral?'

'He hasn't been too well these last few days.'

'God bless him! He's had a good run for his money anyway. Here. Hold on a minute.'

They walked down the platform together.

'Never get in a carriage with a single gent . . . unless of course you know him. Get my meaning?'

He selected a suitable carriage for her and opened the door.

'Hop in.'

Nancy nodded seriously at him and climbed into the train. Two gents were reading their papers and an elderly woman was knitting. She would be perfectly safe. Mr Carroll slammed the door. She pulled down the window and leant out.

'Thank you, Mr Carroll.'

'Mind yourself, Nancy. Mind yourself.'

He put his whistle in his mouth and waved the green flag.

The gents rattled their newpapers and one of them looked at his watch. The woman knitted, one purl, two plain, fingers industrious. With a great expulsion of steam the train jerked forward. Nancy waved at Mr Carroll and he waved the green flag back at her. She pulled up the window and sat down. She drew her initials in the dust on the window as the backs of some shops and then some houses jogged past and then the empty harbour, nets curled by the sea wall. The train gathered speed. The tip of her finger was grey so she wiped it on her skirt.

Clickety clunk, clunkety click, clickety clickety clickety . . .

The woman seemed to be knitting in time to the rhythm of the wheels. She stared out of the window at the sea as her fingers worked. An expert, Nancy thought.

Clickety clickety, mystery, mystery. Occasionally for a few moments the wheels stopped their chattering and seemed to hum. Clickety. What was he doing now, the mystery? Still perhaps sitting on the rug pondering? Perhaps. Clickety, pondering what? The lady began to count stitches, pushing each one carefully along one needle with the tip of the other needle. Her mouth numbered silently. He had a really rather splendid face. Tired. Splendid. Used. A used face. How old? Clickety, clickety. Fifty something. She always found it hard to tell.

The whistle screamed and they rushed into the long tunnel. All she could see was her own unused face in the dusty window haloed with whirling sparks.

Was he mad, she wondered. No. Lying low? Gosh, perhaps he was one of Them! After all, there were a few people like him mixed up with . . . perhaps even Uncle Gabriel if he hadn't been killed wearing the uniform of what was now the other side. If he were one of Them . . . ? Perhaps, on the other hand, he might be a Bolshevist? He didn't look bad, she thought, sadly recalling his face again into her mind – only used, sick. Discretion, he said. I will be silent as the grave.

They rushed out into the light again. Directly below the line the sea was deep and sombre, while out beyond the evening shadow of the hill it sparkled gaily still. In the bay a dozen or so yachts were racing, their white sails filled with wind. Clickety, clickety. Knitting again, fingers dancing, the ball of brown wool bobbing on her knee. One of the gents looked at his watch again and made a tutting face. Impatient. The open fields on the other side had turned now to suburban gardens, neat beds of flowers, tennis courts, carefully patterned rows of vegetables, washing dancing in the wind. Then a deep cutting where you could see nothing, only high stone walls and a peep of sky, and the sound of the wheels became a roar again.

More houses, backyards, glimpses of the sea and then the huge beach at Merrion, stretching almost over to Howth, it seemed, and almost empty now except for a distant flock of birds out near the sea's edge and a few children running with a dog. The train swerved inland again and the houses were pressed closer and closer together, no green. Grimy windows stared as the train went past, grey and red brick, no more trees; here and there lights were already shining from dark rooms. The lady folded up her knitting and put it into her large black bag. The gents rattled their papers together; one of them pleated his neatly and put it into his pocket, the other left his lying on the seat. One of them yawned, the other looked at his watch again.

Clickety clunk. Clunkety click. Click . . . click . . .

Harry was standing on the steps of his office waiting for her.

'Hello, Nancy.' He took off his hat.

'Gosh, I hope you haven't been standing there for ages!'

'No. No. Not at all. Well . . . let's go and catch a bite.'

He put his hat on again and they began to walk along the pavement.

The evening sun flashed in the top windows of the houses. Signals, she thought. Secrets flickering from one street to the next. Sparks crackled from the overhead points as a tram went past. More signals. This evening the city is full of secrets.

He took hold of her elbow and pushed her along the street firmly.

'You look nice. A new get-up?'

She blushed with pleasure.

'I'm just tidy. That's all. Aunt Mary stood threateningly by. She said I looked like a human being for once. Would you agree?'

'Absolutely.'

'An absolutely human bean. What a distinguished thing to be! I'm not a runner bean, or a French bean or even a has been . . .'

'Do shut up, Nancy. Why do you always carry on so!'

'Where's Maeve?'

Fingers crossed tightly in her pocket. Not coming. What bliss! Never coming again. Found beautifully drowned, like Ophelia or the lady who went to call the cattle home across the Sands of Dee. Hair floating, lilies, ever so romantic. What bliss! A beautiful corpse. Aunt Mary would make a beautiful floral tribute, she was very good at that. Twisting and twining the flowers. Much better than ordering some stiff old bunch from a shop. They would all cry at the grave-side. Harry would mourn handsomely for a year and then . . .

'. . . So she's meeting us at the theatre,' he was explaining.

46

'Oh . . . ah . . . yes!' Nancy sighed.

He guided her off the pavement. A slight wind came round the corner and accompanied them across the road. There was a smell of dung and dust. The tramlines were like silver ribbons on the cobbles.

'So I thought we'd have a bite in Bewley's. Quickish, you know. Is that all right?'

She smiled up at him.

'Anything. Golly, anything!'

A lorry full of soldiers came down Dame Street and swung past the Bank of Ireland, heading for the river.

'I suppose they're off to shoot someone,' she suggested in a conversational voice.

Harry frowned but didn't say anything.

She took his arm.

'If you hadn't left the army after the war, you might have been there with them. Going off to shoot someone.'

A tram swayed past, stately ship on rails.

'How would that have appealed to you?'

She tugged at his arm for an answer.

'I'd like to get a few of the bastards.'

He closed his mouth tightly to stop any more words coming out and looked down at his shining black shoes as they moved on the pavement.

'Harry . . . ?'

'That's enough.'

They walked up Grafton Street in silence. As they crossed the road to Bewley's Oriental Café, a motor car driven by a middle-aged man passed in front of them. Nancy leant forward and peered at him as he drove slowly past.

The warm smell of freshly ground coffee seemed to suck them through the swing doors and into the café.

'Do you think that could have been my father?'

Harry looked startled.

'Who? Where?'

'That man back there in the car.'

'Oh, for heaven's sake!'

He pushed her in front of him across the shop and through the door at the back leading into the café itself.

'I always look in passing motors for my father.' She

instantly regretted having said it. She laughed nervously. 'Joke, joke.'

'Sit down.'

He pulled out a chair at a small table for her as he spoke. She sat down. She watched him as he hung his hat on a tall curling hatstand, then unbuttoned his coat with neat careful movements of his hands. At last he, too, sat down, and pushed the menu across the table towards her.

'Your father's dead.'

'How do you know?'

'Everyone knows that, you silly child!'

'I don't.'

'Of course you do. What do you want to eat? We haven't much time.'

'Where is his grave then?'

'Nancy, I . . .'

'Where is there a bit of paper saying that he's dead? Something legal. Mr Robert Gulliver is dead. That sort of thing. Where?'

'How on earth should I know! Ask Mary these silly questions. She's the one who knows the answers.'

Nancy shook her head. Impatiently he tapped his finger on the table and pointed to the menu. She glanced at it.

'I'll have scrambled eggs and potato cakes,' she said, 'and coffee.'

'Sure?'

'Yes, sure.'

He waved at a waitress.

'She only surmises. She has no conclusions to come to.' She leaned towards him. 'My mother's dead. I know that. I have her hairbrush . . . things like that . . . golly, I even sleep in her bed, but Robert . . . he . . . my . . .'

'I should surmise, too, if I were you.'

'Sometimes,' she whispered to herself, as she watched him give their order to the waitress, 'you are such a pain in the neck.'

He scratched for a moment at the corner of his eye with a clean pale finger. His nails were well trimmed and perfect; his hands looked as if they had never even hovered over any of the mess of life.

'I'll tell you one thing, he's not driving round Dublin in a motor, wherever else he may be.'

'You don't know.'

'I, too, can surmise.'

Around them people clattered their knives and forks and stirred the coffee in the heavy white cups and smiled at each other or read the paper. Outside, there was some sort of a war going on, she thought, but here, just sitting in this warm dim room, you would never know it. She looked at the calm faces around her and wondered perhaps if two of those leaning, smiling people, normal people, were plotting to kill someone, passing secret messages as they stirred their coffee, betraying someone, smiling and smiling. The waitress put a plate down in front of her and another in front of Harry, who was looking rather cross; then she shuffled the things on the table round a bit to make room for the coffee pot and a dish of fat, steaming potato cakes.

'I hope that's all right,' said Harry politely.

'Scrumptious.'

'You pour out. You're the lady. I take two lumps of sugar.'

He picked up his knife and fork and began to eat bacon and sausages, cutting them with care, his head bent towards his plate. Her hand shook a little as she poured the coffee, but she didn't spill any into his saucer.

'Am I bore?'

He looked up from his food and smiled at her. For a moment she felt a little dizzy, confronted with his smile.

'You're a silly child,' he said, 'but not a bore. Yet. You could become one if you go on being silly, but I don't suppose you will for long.'

'A blooming bore?'

'Eat your scrambled eggs. We mustn't keep Maeve waiting.'

10 August

Having made the momentous decision to write daily in my book, I find to my disgust that I have been lazy . . . perhaps haphazard would be a better word. I think I am probably a somewhat haphazard person. Maybe this has to do with my age, and one day I will, as Harry hopes so much, become a real person. Organised. Anyway he has no cause for complaint about my behaviour last night. I behaved like a perfect lady. We kept Maeve waiting for a few minutes, but she bore it nobly. She was dressed in pale mauve, a colour I normally find quite disagreeable, but it suited her well.

The two plays we saw were *Androcles and the Lion* by George Bernard Shaw and *Riders to the Sea*. I laughed quite a lot during *Androcles* and cried during *Riders to the Sea*. I suppose these were the right reactions to have. In spite of my laughter I didn't really like Mr Shaw's play very much, but I didn't mention this to Harry and Maeve, who thought it was marvellous.

The Abbey Theatre has a strange smell; perhaps all theatres do, but I have no experience.

We had to hurry to get out of town before the curfew. Maeve sat in the front seat and smiled and chattered and touched Harry's arm with her hand from time to time. We passed several military lorries on our way home, but saw no trouble of any sort. There is really no need to be frightened if you're with Harry; nothing terrible could ever happen to you when you are with him.

They had all gone to bed here when I got home. Aunt Mary had left the light burning in the hall so that I didn't have to come into a dark house. At one end of the long hall table was a tray with a jug of milk, neatly covered with a muslin cloth edged with coloured beads, to keep the flies out, a glass and a plate with a slice of Bridie's loveliest fruit cake, usually kept for visitors. I turned out the light and sat down at the bottom of the stairs.

The house was still and loving. The hall clock ticked and the furniture around me breathed quietly, in the way that furniture does at night when everything is silent. A mouse rattled things in the kitchen and the moon shone in through the fanlight over the hall door and made patterns like orange segments on the floor and up the stairs and indeed probably on me too. I felt very safe, well protected. I wondered was that right or wrong, but didn't come to any conclusions.

It was raining the next afternoon when Nancy went down to the hut. The beach was deserted. The sky and sea were the same turbulent grey; white flashes of foam rose and fell, sighing patterns of unrest. The telegraph poles sang. She carried with her an old school satchel in which she had gathered together an assortment of food.

He was sitting hunched in the corner, his thin shoulders covered by a rug. He held a book in his hand. He laid the book on the floor and got to his feet when she came in.

'I'm sorry,' he said. 'It never occurred to me that you might come today. It's hardly a day for the beach.'

'I brought you some food . . . well, not much really . . . just a few bits and pieces. I wasn't sure how you managed.'

Nervously she squeezed drops of water from the ends of her hair with her fingers as she spoke.

'How thoughtful of you, and kind!'

She held the satchel out towards him. He took it from her and put it on the shelf without opening it.

'You don't have to worry about me, you know. I'm grateful . . . I don't mean that . . . I'm . . . well, very good at managing.'

The stood looking at each other for a long moment.

'Did you enjoy the Abbey?' he asked politely.

51

'It was very good. Thank you.'

'Would you like me to disappear for a while?'

'Oh no! Please, no. I didn't say a word to anyone.'

He smiled slightly.

'About you.'

She stopped torturing her hair and wiped her wet fingers on the front of her skirt.

'I didn't think you would.'

'You never know with people.'

'I think you know all right. Yes. Maybe it's my great age and experience. Why don't we sit down? I have never believed in standing when you can sit.' He spread the rug and cushions out so that there would be room for both of them and then politely waited until she had settled herself before he sat down beside her.

'Well, here we are,' he said.

'Yes.'

He pulled a half-smoked cigarette out of his pocket and pinched some of the burnt end off before putting it in his mouth. Then he fished for matches.

'Are you dying?' she asked suddenly.

He looked startled. He found the matches and struck one. His hands was shaking as he raised the flame towards his face. He shook the match dead before putting the charred stick safely back in the box.

'Not any more than anyone else. Why do you ask?'

'I just thought . . . well . . . wondered . . . it seemed like a possible explanation.'

'Why in the name of God should I choose to come and die here! No, no, Nancy Gulliver, I'd prefer to die in comfort.'

'I don't really think that would enter your head.'

He laughed.

'Rubbish, dear child. I'm no romantic hero. I'm as sybaritic as the next man. Most certainly when it comes to dying. I'd rather die in a warm bed, having just had a good meal and a bottle of claret, than after a couple of green apples on a windy beach.'

'To cease upon the midnight with no pain . . .'

'It's an appealing thought.'

'Grandfather can't die. He just sits there waiting and nothing happens.' She picked at the inside of her nose with the first finger of her right hand. 'I find it very disconcerting . . . well worse than that really. He just waits hopelessly. Yes. We watch him. Each day he shrivels a little, but he won't die.'

'Must you pick your nose?'

She removed her finger rapidly and blushed.

'Sorry. I didn't realise . . .'

'Tell me about yourself. What do you do apart from watching the old man shrivel?'

'I don't really do anything. I'm an orphan.'

'So am I.'

She laughed.

'Silly! I've never had parents.'

'You appeared, in other words, in a puff of smoke, rather like the demon in the pantomime.'

'What fun that would have been!'

'And the grandfather . . .'

'I live with him and my aunt. Over there.'

She pointed vaguely in the direction of the railway line. 'I only left school last term. I'm going to Trinity in the autumn.'

'To read what?'

'History. It seems like quite a good thing to start off with anyway. Aunt Mary says I'll probably get bored with it.'

'And is Aunt Mary given to being right?'

'She really wanted me to go to Oxford, but . . . well . . . we didn't have enough money for that. She says I need intellectual hounding to keep me at work . . . and discipline. She says I probably won't get either here. She says . . .' She stopped and looked anxiously at him.

'Well?'

'She says it's probably all for the best that we haven't the money anyway because if there's going to be a war with England . . . a real war . . . then I'd be better off staying here. After all . . .'

'And does she think there's going to be a real war with England?'

His face was amused.

'She says they're all such fearful muddlers that there might be.'

A gust of wind threw a burst of raindrops on to the roof. They sounded like pebbles landing and then sliding, and then becoming silent.

'She's good.'

'Ah, yes!'

'She's very good to Grandfather, and she's very good to me. To people, really everyone. Her life is full of order. Don't you think that is a good thing?'

'Certainly.'

'You don't say that with conviction.'

'Nancy Gulliver, you must have been a very trying child.'

She smiled slightly.

'In the photographs my mother looks very like her. I'd say she was less ordered though.'

'Why do you think that?'

'She had me.' She leant towards him as if she were afraid of being overheard. 'I suspect she wasn't married. That wasn't very orderly, was it? Mind you, it isn't what people say, it's just what I suspect.'

'Perhaps it would make things easier for you if you believed what they say.'

'Perhaps.'

Overcome with a sudden hunger she got up and took the satchel off the shelf; she peered into it.

'Have a banana?'

'No thanks. I never eat between meals.'

'Do you mind if I have one? There are three there.'

'Go ahead. Help yourself.'

She took out a banana and pulled the peel back carefully. The flesh of the fruit was beginning to turn from cream to pulpy brown. Reluctantly she sat down again, stretching her legs out in front of her. She wanted to move them, pace like a lion backwards and forwards in her cage. Her long second toe poked inquisitively through the wet canvas of her sandshoe. She chewed and gazed at it as if she were alarmed somehow at its appearance. He wondered whether he should pick up his book and continue with his reading.

'What's your name?' she asked after a long, long silence.

'Haven't we had this conversation before?'

'It didn't get us very far. One ought . . . really . . . technically . . . to know one's lodger's name. I mean . . . you're not a . . . but . . . anyway.'

He didn't say a word.

She folded the empty banana skin and put it into her pocket.

'Your name isn't Robert, by any chance?'

'I've had so many names down the years.'

'Was Robert ever one of them?'

'Not that I can recall. It's not really a very interesting name.'

'My father was called Robert.'

He roared with laughter. After a moment she laughed, too, and their laughter and the wind shook the little hut.

'Ah now, ah come on now, Nancy! You're not blaming me for that?'

'Why not? Why not you?'

'How do you know his name is Robert? After all, if you don't believe what they say . . .'

'I know that. Grandfather talks about Robert from time to time, and he's well past telling lies. Anyway. I have this book.' Her fingers stroked an ancient childhood scar on her knee as she spoke. She forever had to be moving. Her hands did not know the meaning of the word peace. 'It's a Yeats first edition. You know, that lovely soft paper and ragged edges where someone has cut the pages with a paper knife . . . He must have given it to her , . . to my mother. It has Helen . . . that was her name.'

The nod of his head could have meant anything or nothing. She wasn't watching him, though; her eyes were scrutinising the black looped writing on the fly-leaf of the book.

' . . . murmur a little sadly how Love fled, And paced upon the mountains overhead, And hid his face amid a crown of stars.'

Silence.

'I don't really know what it means.'

Silence.

'It's nice though ... good. "Helen," it says then "from Robert." So you see.'

'Yes, I see,' he said gently. 'And I assure you it was not I who wrote those words.'

'Oh well.' She spoke with resignation in her voice.

'It shouldn't be so important, you know.'

He bent down and ground out the remains of his cigarette on the sole of his shoe. He held the butt in the hollow of his hand like you might hold a tiny dead animal.

'When you are young, there is today and tomorrow. A lot of tomorrows. It's only when you get to my age that the past begins to play a part in your life. Uninvited. Willy nilly.'

'I'd just like to know what is inside me. What sort of a person I might expect to turn out to be.'

'That's rubbish, child.'

'Surely ingredients must be important?'

'Irrelevant. We can do nothing about them but forget them and get on with the job of maturing, exploring and expanding our faculties.'

'Is that what you've done? I mean, are doing?'

He looked down at the butt in his hand.

'Just throw it on the floor,' she said.

He got up and went over to the door; as he opened it a gust of rain burst its drops on the floor. He threw the butt out on to the sand and shut the door again quickly.

'I'm not what you might call old.' He smiled and corrected himself. 'Not what I might call old, and yet . . . all the time now . . . willy nilly, as I said before, the past impinges on me. Nudges its way constantly into my life. Uninvited. I no longer seem to have time for contemplation. I find it very unnerving. I find I can no longer act unimpeded by voices from the past.'

He was talking to himself, standing quite still by the door, his face a pale blur in the darkness.

'The whole structure of my life begins to tremble, like this funny hut when the wind blows.' He held his hands out in front of him in a sudden gesture, and she saw that they also were trembling. 'So, for the first time in years, everything I do becomes tentative. I have to pretend, fool people. I used to be sure, devastatingly sure; now I have to squash doubts, sharpen constantly the edges of my thoughts. Perhaps to become lost is the fate of the middle-aged and the middle class. It might be compared with the loss of Faith.' He looked at his hands for a moment and then let them fall slowly to his sides. She felt she was eavesdropping.

'Oh dear!' he said. 'I'm sorry. I don't usually meander. Another symptom.'

He came and sat down again beside her.

'I don't mind,' she said. 'I don't know what you're talking about, but I like listening to you.'

'The perfect person to have around.'

He said it gently, without irony.

'I've never had Faith,' she said.

'I expect you will some day, in something or other; even yourself. It doesn't have to be in God, you know.'

'I often wonder if it helps . . . Faith in God, I mean. Does it make life easier? Less . . . well . . . full of dark corners?'

'I'm afraid not. I'm not really a God man myself, so I wouldn't like to mislead you. I can say with conviction, though, that it's very important to feel you have a reason for being alive.'

'I've always hated caves. When we used to go on picnics . . . when I was . . . well young . . . you know . . . a . . .'

He nodded encouragingly.

'They all used to go rushing into any caves that might be around. Hurray, they'd shout, lovely lovely caves! I couldn't bear it. I used to stay outside. I could hear them calling and laughing inside. I knew I was missing something, but I couldn't go in. They used to tease me when they came out. You sometimes find terrible things in caves.'

'True.'

'And mazes and locked rooms that haven't been opened for years and cellars. And dark secret passageways. I hate being frightened.'

'You seem to have no sense of adventure. Most young people get a thrill from being scared. They sometimes even find it stimulating. Not you?'

'No.'

'What do you get a thrill from?'

She thought for a moment, gnawing nervously at a finger-nail.

'I like throwing stones into the sea.'

'A noble occupation.'

'Sarcasm,' she said angrily. 'I'm trying to tell you. I think I must be a mutt of some sort. Words. I get a thrill from words. Written, spoken, words just jumbling themselves round in my head . . . hardly even thought, like shadows, but making their own noise. Do you understand?'

'I think you're probably in for a hard time, young woman.'

'I'm starting out with a lot of advantages.'

'Yes. But you must realise that sometimes those advantages can get very much in the way.'

There was a long silence between them. A gull landed on the roof. They could hear its claws scraping impatiently on the wood until it found a position to its liking.

'And yet,' he said eventually. 'You're not afraid of me?'

'Should I be?'

'I am as unknown to you as a locked room might be.'

'People don't frighten me. Only the very clever ones who seem to know everything.'

'But you must know they don't.'

'I feel they can't really, but I'm never sure.'

He put his hand into his pocket and pulled something out. He held it out towards her. It was a gun.

Inside her stomach some very disagreeable thing jumped. She neither moved nor spoke until whatever it was had settled itself back into its appointed place again. Her heart was beating very fast.

'Well?'

'Is that all you're going to say?'

'What do you want me to say?' Her voice was angry, rather shrill. May I live, may I live, may I live!

'Are you going to kill me or . . . something?'

'Of course not.' He put the gun back into his pocket.

'Why . . . why . . .?'

'I carry a gun. I just suddenly thought you ought to know.'

'You . . . have you . . .?'

'I use it if I have to.'

58

He put his hand once more into his pocket and she braced herself to see the gun again, but he took out his cigarettes instead. He took one from the box and tapped it for a moment on his thumb before putting it into his mouth.

'I make no apologies if I have upset you.' The cigarette nodded in the corner of his mouth as he spoke. 'The first fact of life you have to grasp if you want to get anywhere at all is that life isn't full of sweetness and light and gentlemen standing up when ladies come into the room. On the contrary, it's full of violence, injustice and pain. That's what you're afraid of seeing when you open those locked doors, peer into caves. The terrible truth.'

'No,' she said. 'No, no . . . oh . . . !'

'Once upon a time . . .' His hand groped again in his pocket, this time for the matches. 'They gave me a lovely uniform and a gun and exhorted me to go and kill the enemies of the people. I did my duty. I was a damn good soldier, Nancy, probably because I don't really have a fear of dying . . . I know that sounds grandiose, but it's true; my fear would be of being trapped by eternal life, like your grandfather . . . I became a major. I was no heroic child, like so many poor fools, just galloping into middle age. Four bloody years in a Field Artillery brigade. I watched men die for what some of them thought were the rights of the small nations. Slaughter. Young men, old men, heroes and devils and just poor sods who thought they were doing their duty.' He struck a match and the flame was reflected in his eyes. Three flames trembled. 'I thought at first we might be striking a million blows for justice. A purge of some sort might be taking place, but of course I was wrong . . . One thing I learnt though.' He shook out the flame on the match and in his eyes and took a deep pull on his cigarette. 'I know the true enemies of the people. The true enemies.' He laughed suddenly. 'I suppose you think I'm a little touched?'

'You could be.' She spoke cautiously. 'A little.'

'I probably am. Ranting. Spouting mumbo-jumbo foolishness at a young person who may never care, never be ruffled . . . by . . . by . . . after all, why should you?'

Smoke began to trickle out through his nose and mouth. She stared at his thin face. Dying, she thought viciously, soon; I hope you die soon. The cigarette drooped between his fingers, hardened by years of pulling the trigger.

'My war,' he said the words gently, 'will never end.'

She stood up

'The sooner you get away out of here the better and . . . and . . . don't think I'll bring you any more bananas . . . or anything. I jolly well won't.'

He leaned his head back against the wall and laughed.

'It's no laughing matter. Get away. Go away. You . . .'

'I don't mean to offend you. Believe me, I'm sorry. I just find things funny.'

'Don't you realise that I will probably go the the police. The army . . . we . . . know officers in the . . .'

'I don't mean to sound patronising, but you go ahead and do that, if you feel you have to. That's all right with me.'

She walked across the room and opened the door. Rain and wind burst turbulently in. The gull on the roof, disturbed by her movement, shifted its position. Its feet clawed impatiently, waiting for calmness again. She turned and looked back at the man. He leant against the wall still, a smile on his face.

'Goodbye.'

'Do you want to take your bananas with you?'

'Shut up! You damn . . . damn . . . !'

She climbed up on to the railway line and walked down the line without looking back. Far out on the horizon a ship ploughed its way towards England. It looked like hard work, pushing its way through the grey rising sea. The sand rose in sheets and flew along the beach before the wind. The sleepers were slippery and the deep cracks in them were filled with water.

Aunt Mary was crossing the hall as Nancy came in through the door. In one hand she held a cup of tea and in the other a plate of thin fingers of hot buttered toast.

'My dear child, you're soaking. Where have you been? Run up and change at once or you'll be all aches and pains tomorrow.'

'Tea . . .' suggested Nancy.

'Don't argue. If you're quick, the tea'll still be drinkable, it's only just made. Your grandfather's actually asked for toast. It's amazing. He's so much better today, the pet. Such a relief.'

'I'll bring a cup up with me.'

'You shouldn't dilly dally round when you're wet like that.'

Nancy went into the drawing-room and poured herself a cup of tea. The pyramid of turf in the fireplace smouldered gently. She cut a piece of sponge cake and went back out into the hall. Aunt Mary was still there.

'There was something . . . ' she said vaguely. 'Look at those drips on the floor, dear. Bridie will be most upset. Drip, drip.'

'Something?'

'Where is death's sting?' sang out the old man from his room across the hall.

'Coming, pet. Toast. Now what was it?'

'I hate that blooming old hymn.'

'Where grave thy victory?'

'Just this moment.' She moved towards the door. 'Harry, ah yes. That's it.'

'Harry?' Nancy's mouth was full of cake.

'He telephoned. Luckily I wasn't in the garden . . . all that rain. I should have been, it's beginning to look like a jungle. I never hear the telephone when I'm in the garden . . . well, I do really, but Mrs Burke is so aggravating, she'll never ring more than twice and you rush huffing and puffing to the dreadful machine and she'll say . . . I didn't think anyone was in, Miss Dwyer. She knows perfectly well there's always somebody in. No patience. It's not even as if she were madly busy. I suppose she can't bear to tear herself away from all the fascinating calls she listens to.'

'Harry . . . ?'

She dropped a piece of cake on the carpet and stooped to pick it up.

'I triumph still if Thou abide with me.'

'Oh yes. He and Maeve are expecting you to dinner. Sevenish. Her parents are going up to town to some function or other and Maeve is entertaining Harry and you to dinner. Something like that.'

'And you said yes . . . Honestly, Aunt Mary!'

'I thought you'd want to go, dear.'

'How exasperating! How . . . bloody!'

'Swearing is very unbecoming in one so young.'

Nancy kicked angrily at the banisters. The tea slopped over the side of her cup into the saucer.

'He sounded very pressing. Have a nice hot bath, dear, there's no point in laying yourself open to rheumatism.'

'He needs me there as . . . well as . . . sort of . . .'

'Ballast. You'll take all the paint off if you go on doing that.'

'There's hardly any paint left on anyway. It's all so beastly shabby.'

Aunt Mary sighed. She suddenly looked forlorn and very tired standing there with the toast cooling rapidly in one hand.

'Isn't it your bridge afternoon anyway?'

'I just thought I'd stay with him. I'd have done some gardening only . . . the rain . . . It wasn't really necessary to stay, but . . .' She looked up at the ceiling and surprisingly whistled a few tuneless notes. 'Mrs Heslop was very put out. You know what she's like . . . but there you are.' She moved a couple of steps towards the door of the old man's room. 'I think he's better, much, much better.' She pushed at the door with her empty hand. 'Perhaps he'll outlive us all. Seven, Harry said. Do run along, dear, and get into that bath.'

She went into the room and closed the door behind her.

'Oh well!' said Nancy to the empty hall.

The bathroom smelt of witch hazel and warm dry linen. Wisteria had crawled its way in through the small window. Nancy lay and stared at the twisted stems of the plant as they worried their way towards the ceiling. There couldn't be many people who had wisteria growing in their bathroom. That was always her routine thought as she lay down in the hot steaming water, and then she forgot about it.

'I will go to the police,' she said to her sponge. It made no comment.

'I am glad after all that he isn't, can't be, my father.

62

Can't be. Deliriously glad. He could be. What am I talking about?'

Her pale untouched body glimmered in the green light.

'Oh sponge, what would you do?'

A drip from the cold tap landed on her big toe. She moved her leg sideways and ripples distorted the shape of her legs.

'Why can't I think straight? Why?' In a moment of rage she threw the sponge across the room. It hit the wall by the basin and fell wetly on to the floor.

'It's all I ask, to be able to come to tidy conclusions. Well, almost all. I am biologically, psychologically, physiologically a mess. Blooming mess.'

She glared across the room at the blameless sponge and then felt better. Aunt Mary's knuckles banged on the door.

'Nancy, pet, not too long lolling in the boiling water. So bad for the skin. It will dry up. Pits and wrinkles.'

So, Nancy scowled, you bully me into the bath, now you bully me out. That's life.

'Anyway time is running on. I'd like to come in. I have to wash my teeth.

Aunt Mary had impulses to wash her teeth at all sorts of odd hours of the night and day. She had little gold fillings in the back of her mouth that you could see when she laughed; perhaps it was important to keep such valuable assets up to the mark.

'Well, come on in. I've nothing to hide.'

'Tut!'

Nancy heard the landing floor creak as she moved away.

'Aunt Mary.'

'Out child, out. You're not even washing. I can hear the silence of total inaction. Out.'

With a sigh Nancy stood up and reached for her towel.

'Are all informers rats?'

The creaking started again, as Aunt Mary came back towards the door.

'I didn't quite hear what you said.'

'Informers? Are they?'

'What a curious question!'

'Have you an answer?'

Silence.

Nancy wriggled the plug out with her big toe. Water rattled down the pipe.

'Well . . . I've often wondered about Judas, you know. I find it hard to accept that for all these centuries he's been regarded as the most despicable man in the world.' There was more silence through the door as Aunt Mary thought about Judas. 'You see . . . maybe he was a hero. I mean, maybe even the greater hero of the two. Terribly strong, far-sighted, the true ally. I only say maybe.'

'I'm sure that's blasphemy or something.'

No thunderbolt. Just the creaking of old dry boards.

'Get a move on, dear child. My teeth are aching to be washed.'

'You haven't answered my question.'

'It's an impossible question to answer. Circumstances are never the same. Sometimes it would be terribly silly not to inform, if that's the word you want to use, other times one wouldn't do it for love nor money. In this country the word informer has rather nasty connotations. Why do you ask such a question anyway?'

'I was just wondering about this and that.'

'Well, wonder about them somewhere else.'

Nancy rubbed herself fiercely with the towel and watched with interest the tiny white flakes of skin that she scoured off her body.

'I wouldn't do it,' she said.

'What's that?' shouted Aunt Mary through the door.

'Nothing.'

As a gesture to the formality of the occasion, she decided to approach the Caseys' house by the wrought iron gate, the swept path, the front door. She walked sedately down the avenue and along the road, wearing her best shoes and stockings and her black crepe dress that Aunt Mary hadn't wanted her to buy because she said it was too old for her. She felt old as she walked . . . well, older anyway. She stretched her neck, swan-like, as they had been implored to do at dancing class. 'Heads in the clouds girls, up, up, up. Grow.' She grew as she walked. She must be six feet tall. She gazed disdainfully at the dusty road, at the silver buckles

on her best shoes. The rain clouds had blown away and the
sky was a luminous greeny-blue. Even from Nancy's great
height you couldn't see the sea, but you could always smell
the sharp breath of salt in the air; sometimes if you were
feeling undignified and put your tongue out, you could even
imagine you could taste it.

As she pushed open the Caseys' gate, her disdain and her
height dwindled a little. Perhaps Aunt Mary had been right
about the dress after all. Maybe she just looked silly in it.
She walked slowly up the path towards the hall door.
Harry's motor was parked outside the garage. Maybe he
would drive her home in it after dinner and she could just
sit there silently beside him and not say anything idiotic or
immature. Glass panels on each side of the door glowed
with light. She put her finger on the bell. She thought of the
man who wasn't Robert and wondered if he were all right.
Had he decided to go? She took her finger off the bell. A
figure moved in the hall. She turned and ran down the path,
scattering gravel on to the neat edges as she ran.

'Nancy . . .' Harry's voice called her name.

She ran out of the gate on to the road.

'Nancy . . .'

Once she had safely turned the corner on to the main
road that led to the railway arch, she stopped running and
walked on as sedately as she could manage. Every pulse in
her body seemed to be bumping at a different rate. The
shoes and stockings and the black crepe dress now were
irrelevant. They would murder her, she thought, but that
would be tomorrow. Now, it was important to stop him
leaving. If he went, she knew he would never come back, but
disappear totally as he must have done so many times in his
life before. Gun or no gun, she didn't want that. By the
railway bridge she climbed over the fence at the bottom of
the embankment. The grass in the field was long and wet
around her ankles. She pulled off her shoes and stockings
and left them by the fence. She clambered up on to the line
and began to walk towards the point. The slipping sun was
gold and its long rays coloured the unfolding waves.

Up on the hill she could see the light shining from the
dining-room window. Aunt Mary and the old man would be

sitting there in silence, worn-out thoughts humming gently in their heads. The tapping of their knives and forks on their plates would be the only sound in the room. The sleepers were wet under her feet. It was strange, she thought, that silence, which was, after all, merely an emptiness in the air, could have such a powerful effect. Presumably the old man led some strange comforting life inside himself that no one could touch, evading even Aunt Mary's gentle watchfulness. You sometimes got tiny splinters of wood in your bare feet, the devil to get out, and if you allowed them to work their way into your bloodstream, they whirled round inside you and eventually pierced your heart. And that was that. A boy and a girl walked on the beach below her. More silence. Their hands were knotted together, their faces looked exhausted by their emotions. Loving was such a problem.

You couldn't make a rhythm as you walked along the tracks, as the sleepers were not a proper stride apart and you had to keep shortening yours to avoid stepping on the sharp little stones between the wood. Sometimes in the summer you could see dolphins, way out near the horizon, their bodies arching and shining as they played. Sssssh! The sea broke the silence and begged for more in one long breath.

When she got to the point, she climbed down from the line and walked along the sand. Here the only marks were the criss-cross patterns made by the birds along the edge of the sea.

He was sitting with his back to the hut, reading. He looked up from the book as she approached, then he got to his feet and stood there looking at her, the book held loosely in his right hand.

'I didn't expect you back quite so soon. I was going to leave in the morning.'

She shook her head.

'I thought maybe . . . perhaps . . .'

'First thing. In the morning.'

'I'm sorry. That's what I came to say. Please don't go.'.

He stared at her in silence for a long time. She felt her face getting red.

'I haven't done anything awful.'

'Sssssh!' said the sea.

'I was afraid you might have gone. I hurried . . .'

The thousand-year-old seagull flew in from the sea and settled on the roof.

'Please don't go.'

'Do you understand what that means?'

'I will try.'

He nodded.

'I think we might have a drink. I take it you're not too young to have a drink?'

'I'd love a drink.'

'I only have whisky.'

'Whisky sounds lovely.' What would Aunt Mary say?

'In or out?'

'Out. Always out, unless it's raining.'

'I'll get a rug.'

'Don't bother. I'm all right.'

'I'll get a rug.'

He went into the hut.

Just like Aunt Mary, fuss, fuss about piles and draughts and rheumatism. All grown-ups were blooming well the same in the end. She did a little whirl around and her black dress flew out like birds' wings. Nice. She whirled again. He came out of the hut with a bottle and two cups and the rug draped round his shoulders.

'What a pretty dress!' he said.

She blushed.

'Oh . . . do you really like it?'

'I do. It makes you look like a young witch. I don't mean the hook-nosed variety who fly around on broomsticks. Perhaps I should say sorceress.'

'Oh!'

She watched him spread the rug on the sand.

'Aunt Mary doesn't like it.'

'For once Aunt Mary doesn't know what she's talking about. Won't you sit down?'

He gestured her to sit down and when she was settled he handed her a cup with a small amount of whisky in it.

'It has to be neat, I'm afraid. My digs don't boast a tap.'

67

'I don't mind,' she said. 'I've never tasted whisky before.'
She frowned into the cup.

'Easy does it,' he said and sat down beside her.

'I love it when the stars are coming out and the sky is still blue.'

'So you came all the way back.'

'Well . . . yes . . . I wondered what I ought to do and then I thought it wasn't my business anyway and I suppose I'm not really old enough to understand about . . . things . . . things. I haven't thought much yet. Anyway I stood at the door and I saw someone coming to open it and I thought I couldn't stand being there all evening and being polite and knowing they didn't really want me. Even in my best clothes I didn't feel . . . adequate . . . I can't bear sitting watching them holding hands . . . metaphorically, I mean.' She stared up at the stars in the blue sky. 'I'm jealous. I hate that. I really do.'

She took a quick sip of her whisky. It was very strong and made the inside of her mouth tingle.

'Do you expect me to have understood all that?'

'Maybe you could just listen and not insist on understanding.'

He smiled faintly and turned away from her, looking out towards the horizon. His face was deeply lined and the skin around his eyes was stretched and wan.

'What age are you?'

'I'm supposed to be listening, not answering questions. Damn fool questions.'

'What am I going to do with my life?'

'That's another damn fool question. Very few people know at your age. A handful do, people born with a bloody purpose. By and large man has to pick up the use of his functions as he goes along. It's important to understand that. The young have no patience.'

'When this war is over . . . what will happen then?'

He laughed.

'There'll be another one . . . I mean the people fighting together now will fight each other. It always happens like that.'

She took another sip from her cup.

'Then the people who win will sit on their thrones and exploit everyone, just the way they've been exploited before. It will be very sad and little progress will have been made. Some people will still have too much to eat and others not enough.'

'It all seems very pointless. Why do you do it?'

'Me? I'm not fighting specifically against the British, I hope I'm fighting for the people. I don't want power, I want to see justice for everyone and I'm prepared to kill anyone who seriously threatens . . .'

She shivered. He put out a hand and touched her shoulder.

'I'm sorry.'

'That's all right. It's just all this killing business. I hate it so much.'

'There are worse things than killing going on in the world. Terrible crimes are committed against people all the time. By other people.'

He took a deep drink.

'The only thing to do is fight.'

'It all sounds very peculiar to me.'

'Yes, I think we'll talk about something else.'

'We live up there on the hill.'

He nodded.

'I know. I told you, I knew this place when I was a child. This . . . this . . .'

He banged with his knuckles on the wall behind them. 'We used to come down here nearly every day. We came in the pony trap with our governess, to play on the beach.'

'We . . .?'

'Yes. We. The children. I remember it so well. Each time I come out of the hut in the morning I remember it all again. Empty sky and beach. Empty sea. And the trains. The driver would lean out and wave to us as he went by. Then it was time to go home for lunch. She always let us stay until the train had passed.' It was dropping into darkness; up behind the line of hills would be black now. 'That was a long time ago. Before . . .'

'Before . . . ?'

'Before I became the person I am now.' He laughed. 'A

truly seedy revolutionary.'

'Did you know my mother?'

'She would only have been a baby. Our world was very small. Even then there wasn't much future for it. I was born in 1870.'

'Gosh!' She counted in her head.

'On Easter Day. A lovely day to be born, when our world was full of daffodils and bells ringing and no one had heard of James Connolly or Patrick Pearse.'

'Grandfather's eighty something. Four I think. He fought in the Crimea.'

'I don't suppose I'll reach such an exalted age.'

'You're ill? I knew you were ill.'

He laughed.

'I am disinclined.'

'I'm sure Grandfather's disinclined, to, but it doesn't get him anywhere. He's cold, as if he were dead already. A dead hand couldn't be colder than his. To touch him makes you shiver. He just sits there covered with rugs and watches the trains go by. He has these field glasses . . . he says he saw my father the other day.'

She put the cup to her mouth and carefully watched him over the top of it.

'Oh!' His face and voice were noncommittal.

'He's potty really.'

'He must be. Aren't you getting cold?'

'A little. Crossing the field towards the railway. It could have been . . . Did you know my Uncle Gabriel?'

'Shall we go inside?'

'No.'

She stood up abruptly and handed him the cup.

'I must go home. I will have music to face.'

'What have you been up to?'

'It was like I told you.'

'You didn't really tell me anything.'

'I ran away from Harry and Maeve.' She grinned. 'For the second time.'

'The pair who metaphorically hold hands all the time?'

'Yes.'

'You could hardly be blamed for that.'

'Aunt Mary will say I was rude.'

'Yes.'

'A lecture on basic elementary manners.'

'And very good for you too. I am old-fashioned enough to believe in good manners.'

'Even when you kill someone?'

'I consider that remark to be very rude.'

'Yes. I'm sorry.'

'It's almost dark, Will you be all right walking home on your own?'

'I don't mind the dark. I'm used to it.'

She held out her hand towards him. He smiled up at her.

'Such formality!' He touched the palm of her hand with his fingers.

'What's your name?'

He grinned.

'You never give up, do you?'

'I'd like to be able to think of you as someone. Not just that man.'

'X?'

She shook her head.

'Too geometric, and not very original.'

'It's a matter of complete indifference to me what I'm called. Labels are what you put on parcels to make sure they get to their destinations.'

'What did your mother call you?'

'I don't remember.'

'Liar.'

She turned and walked away from him. The sand was beginning to feel cold. A rising wind was singing in the telegraph wires along the railway. The seagull, settled for the night, stared into space. She had a sudden desire to clap her hands or yell, and see its startled flight. It would have been unkind. The sea was restless. She stopped on one of the granite blocks and called back to him. 'I know what I will call you.'

'What would that be, Miss Gulliver?'

'Cassius.'

'Charming.' His voice was ironic.

'Because you have a lean and hungry look.'

71

'He came to a sticky end. But remember . . . "so often shall the knot of us be called the men that gave their country liberty".'

'Who said that?'

'Caius Cassius.'

'The beastly conspirator.'

'Run along and face the music.'

'Will you be here . . .?'

'Who can tell? It is probable.'

'Good night, Cass.'

She climbed on up to the line and began to walk along the sleepers.

'Good night, Miss Gulliver.'

She retrieved her damp shoes and stockings and walked barefoot along the road towards home and retribution.

'Wu . . . hoo!' called a friendly owl as she turned in the gate. The moon smirked from the centre of an empty sky.

'Yoo-hoo!' answered Nancy.

'To who?'

'To you, silly thing.'

Impenetrable banks of rhododendrons bordered the avenue, with brambles climbing their way up through the branches and bursting out, covering the tops of the bushes with alien white flowers. Light shone through a crack in the drawing-room curtains.

'Wu-hoo!'

'Good night, owl. Wish me luck.'

The brass knob was cold in the palm of her hand as she turned it. She thought of his warm fingers.

Aunt Mary was standing in the drawing-room door.

'Honestly, Nancy . . . words fail me!'

Nancy followed her into the room. The old man was sitting in his chair smiling to himself about something that had happened a hundred years before. Harry was sitting opposite him, his long legs stretched out across the fire-place. No smile there, not even a flicker. Aunt Mary stood in the middle of the room and looked exasperated.

'Honestly, Nancy . . . !' began Harry.

'Aunt Mary's already said that.'

'You have been very rude, Nancy. There is no need for more rudeness.'

'Sorry.'

'So you should be.'

Aunt Mary moved towards the old man's chair and gripped the back of it.

'I am going to put Father to bed.'

'Bed,' said Grandfather. 'Am I going to bed?'

'It's late, pet. You're tired.'

'I am not tired, Mary. Sometimes . . . just sometimes I like to be able to make my own decisions.'

'Medicine and things. I'll rub your back. If you're good I'll read to you. A little read. I too am tired.'

'I may not be able to sleep.'

'Of course you'll sleep, Father.'

'I can't ever sleep. I just lie there. What's the point of going to bed, if I just lie there in the dark?'

'Hush, dear. It'll be all right. Apologise, Nancy. You really must do that, you know.'

'And then to still be awake when it starts to get light. It's unbearable, Mary.'

'I'll rub your back Father dear . . .'

The door swung closed behind them.

Nancy turned to Harry.

'I'm sorry.'

She sat down on the arm of the sofa and looked at her bare feet. Strands of grass and tiny stones clung to their dampness.

'I simply don't understand you, Nancy.'

She shrugged her shoulders slightly.

'I mean to say . . . you never think of people . . . poor Maeve . . . I mean, I know you, but what is she . . . to think?'

'I just can't bear the thought of sitting there all evening looking at you two mooning at each other.'

'We do not moon at each other.'

'That is a matter of opinion.'

He picked up the poker and banged at a piece of wood in the fire angrily; it hissed at him like a cat.

'You'll have to grow up soon. Learn to behave. I've said it before . . .'

'And you'll say it again. I'm hungry.'

She rubbed her hand over her flat, empty stomach.

'I'm angry. How can you expect people to treat you nicely?'

'I don't.'

He chewed at his lower lip as he looked across the room at her. His exasperated blue eyes flickered slightly as they focused on her face.

'I must go and find some food. I might collapse at any moment. Die, oh Lord, die, my belly sticking to my backbone!'

She sucked in her cheeks and looked skull-like at him. He didn't show any signs of smiling. She moved towards the door; he got up and followed her.

'You've upset Mary too.' The sound of their footsteps filled the stone passage.

'She was shocked when I told her, really shocked. Upset.'

'Why did you tell her? Tell tale tit. Informer. That's what you are.'

'Don't be silly! I thought you might have been taken ill or something. Or . . .'

'Run away with the milkman.'

She lifted her right fist and banged on the kitchen door, then she threw the door open and switched on the light all in one rather confused movement.

'Wah!'

The kitchen smelt of ironed clothes and fresh bread.

'What's all that in aid of?'

'Mice,' she said, stepping cautiously through the door and looking round. 'I always hope to scare them away. Attack, you know, is the best form of defence. As an old military man you should know that.'

'Gosh, are you afraid of mice?'

'Don't sneer. We all have our problems.'

'Anyway, there's the cat.'

A large orange cat was pretending to be asleep in the pool of light in the middle of the kitchen table.

'He likes mice. They're his friends. He wouldn't dream of hurting a mouse. He's too blooming well fed.'

She lifted the lid of the bread crock and looked in.

'Have some bread and jam? Nice brown bread and raspberry jam.'

'I've eaten,' he said coldly.

'Oh yes. A piece of cake? Do sit down. Bridie always hides the cake, but I bet I could find it if you wanted some. A healthy glass of milk?'

'Nancy . . .'

'The cat has yellow eyes. Well, sort of yellow. They match his fur. Orangey-yellow. Isn't it amazing?'

'Nancy . . .'

'I always think that only very evil people have yellow eyes, witches,' she smiled suddenly. 'Sorcerers. Such-like. Wouldn't you agree?'

'Nancy . . .'

'For heaven's sake sit down, Harry! You're making me nervous. That's why I keep talking such nonsense.'

She opened the press and took out some yellow butter on a plate.

'I won't say another word until you sit down.'

A pot of jam, a knife, a plate. In silence she put them on the table. The table was pale and grained and glowed with much scrubbing. The cat's tail quivered for a moment and then the end of it flipped, striking the table a hard blow. Nancy cut a piece of bread and then sat down. Her hands moved in the light. The rest of her, face and body, was shadowy, almost invisible.

Harry rattled a chair across the flags and sat down opposite her. 'Why do you wear black?'

Her hands moved busily.

'Young people shouldn't wear black. Something bright, gay, pretty.'

'I like it.'

'Black is . . . well . . . I'm not saying you don't look nice . . . but . . . Maeve thought so too. Black she said . . .'

'I'd like to be beautiful.' She took a bite of bread and jam and chewed at it for a moment. Beads of raspberry jam stuck to her lips. 'Burn the topless towers of Ilium. Nothing less would do.'

'I can't get a word you're saying. Your mouth is full.'

'Sweet Helen make me immortal with a kiss.'

75

'You and your Shakespeare.'

She looked at him with amusement and said nothing. Just chewed.

'Where did you run off to anyway?'

She licked her sticky lips.

'Just along the beach for a walk. I felt so odd. It was so beautiful after all that rain. Still. Shriven.'

'What an odd word to use!'

'It just came to me. Purified. It must be marvellous to feel like that . . . like sometimes you find white bones. Lovely white smooth bones.'

She began to cut another piece of bread.

'I often wonder if you feel purified after making love. Absolutely purified. It must have some sort of effect like that on you. Does it?'

She pointed the bread knife at him across the table. To his annoyance he felt his face getting red.

'I don't know,' he muttered.

'Crumbs!' she said.

She buttered the bread and spread some more jam on it. The cat, for some reason of its own, began to purr; otherwise the silence might have been alarming.

'I'd better go,' he said eventually.

She didn't appear to have heard him. She licked some jam off the end of the knife.

'You mean you've never . . . never . . . well . . . ?'

She leaned forward into the light and stared somewhat severely at him.

'You've never . . . you know . . . ?'

'You're idiotic,' he said crossly. 'I refuse to answer questions like that.'

'Fucked?' Malicious voice.

He got to his feet and stood looking silently down at her.

'How extraordinary! You're so old.'

'Mary . . .'

'Oh you can tell her this too. Only you wouldn't dare. I know all sorts of words like that.'

'You're a dreadful little brat.'

'Haven't you even got the curiosity to try? I suppose you won't tell me truthfully.'

'Mary should have sent you to a decent boarding school. My parents always thought that too.'

She burst out laughing.

'Standards, manners, traditional . . .' His voice petered out at the sound of her laughter. 'You know what I mean.'

'Lovely sacred moo cows.'

'I'm going now.' He moved towards the door. 'You'll have a word with Maeve tomorrow . . . explain . . . apologise . . .'

She didn't reply. Half light, half shadow, like a ghost she sat, and the cat opened its yellow eyes and stared at him.

'You will, won't you?'

'Maeve.' She sighed.

'Of course you will.' He spoke the words without conviction.

He opened the door and stood looking at her

'I'll tell you one thing,' she said. 'I'll have done it by the time I'm twenty-six.'

He slammed the door and hurried down the passage. She listened to his feet on the flagstones rushing him away from her.

'I really want him to love me,' she said to the cat. The silly orange brute didn't care. 'I'm crying.' She touched her cheek with a finger. 'If I really were a sorceress, cat, I'd make him love me, but then that wouldn't be fair.' The cat adjusted its position slightly and went to sleep. Nancy rubbed at the tears with the sleeve of the black dress, then she got up and put the bread, the jam and the butter back carefully in their places. She wiped the crumbs off the table into the palm of her hand and went and threw them into the sink, mainly to discourage the mice, but also to placate the mild anger of Bridie, who was never at her best in the morning. The cat's tail trembled as she turned out the light and left the room.

12 August

Looking back at things, I feel that perhaps my small glass of whisky was to be blamed for my behaviour to Harry and my subsequent tears. I feel extraordinarily tired and rather hot in the head. It has been a rather curious day. I have never seen a gun at such close proximity before. The soldiers carry them, of course, and people hang them on their walls as somewhat bizarre decoration; I also remember that Uncle Gabriel used to go shooting, but somehow those guns have never had any direct connection with me before. The one he held in his hand so close to me made me very frightened. He has none of my features; I examine them minutely when I think he isn't watching me. I wonder what he looked like when he was my age, way back in the last century. Anyway, common sense tells me that it would be a ridiculous coincidence to meet one's father under such circumstances. I still wonder. I also wonder what happens to all the certainty you have when you are young . . . very young, he would say. I used to be so positive, I knew so much. Miss Know All, Bridie would call me when she got too exasperated with me. It all drains away, leaving you alone, like standing on the top of a mountain with a cold wind blowing. No protection. I wonder, do other people feel this desolation? Aunt Mary says I think too much about myself. Desolation, isolation. Harry would never feel like this. I think that must be why I love him. He is truly safe and beautiful. Beautiful Harry. I would love to see how his body looks when he is naked, coming out of the sea, shining with wetness and drops running from his hair down over his face and shoulders. I have only seen children's bodies, and my own, of course, which isn't exactly awe-inspiring. Curiosity killed the cat, Aunt Mary would say. Aunt Mary is right about a lot of things.

The next morning was brilliant very early. The sun crept under Nancy's sleeping eyelids long before seven. She could hear the swallows rattling under the eaves and the early morning cooing of a pigeon. Above her head the cracks tracing their way across the white plaster of the ceiling turned into the face of the man on the beach. Up till that moment the cracks had always formed a picture of an old woman with a watering can, but now she had disappeared and he stared gravely at the window.

'An omen,' said Nancy sleepily, being at an age when omens were of great importance. She pulled the sheet up over her face and went to sleep again. When she woke again about an hour later, the birds were in full song and she could hear the water from Aunt Mary's bath gurgling down through the pipes. The old woman was back in her place, watering eternally at nothing.

In the dining room Aunt Mary had the paper neatly folded and propped against the coffee pot.

'Good morning.' She raised her cheek slightly for a kiss, but didn't take her eyes from the page in front of her. It was the racing page, quite incomprehensible to Nancy.

'Why don't you read the news?' Nancy sat down and began to peel an orange.

'Coffee?' Aunt Mary put the paper down beside her plate and picked up the coffee pot. She poised it somewhat threateningly over Nancy's cup.

'Please.'

'I never read the news on racing days. Such terrible things keep on happening.' She replaced the coffee pot on its stand and propped the paper up again. 'I like to enjoy myself on racing days. It's perfectly simple.'

The waving branches of the trees, which now stretched themselves too close to the windows, made shadow patterns on the wall.

Bridie tapped through the hall with her broom, brushing

yesterday's dust out into the garden, from where it had come in the first place.

Aunt Mary put little dabs of butter and marmalade on her toast before each bite, an operation she was able to perform without taking her eyes from the paper.

'Some people,' said Nancy, just to be annoying, 'say that gambling is a sin.'

'There are some people who would say that sitting still and breathing is a sin. Did you sort things out with Harry?'

'Sort of.'

'A little politeness is important.' She sighed. 'I suppose I haven't brought you up very well.'

'Don't be silly. I'm beautifully brought up. I don't eat peas off my knife or belch in public and then say pardon. Even Bridie thinks I'm not too bad. I just . . . well . . . have my own limitations.'

'I do wish you'd take milk in your coffee. It's so bad for your heart like that.'

'We don't talk much, do we?'

'I wouldn't say that, dear.'

'We say things to each other, make a noise, but we don't talk. People who live in the same house hardly ever seem to talk to each other. Who do you talk to?'

Aunt Mary looked a little alarmed.

'I have friends . . .'

'Oh I know . . . I know that. You have your bridge friends and your racing friends and the people you knew in your childhood days and all that. That's not what I mean. Don't you ever need to tear yourself open and get out all that stuff that's burning you inside?'

'You sound as if you need a surgeon rather than a friend. Tut! It's part of the mythology of youth that people go round burning themselves up inside. It's not like that at all, pet. Most people lead and want to lead calm, equilibrious . . .' She laughed and repeated the word . . . 'equilibrious lives.' She reached out and touched Nancy's hand. 'There's no point in making life more difficult than it has to be.'

There was a long silence. Aunt Mary began to gather up her letters, read and neatly tucked back into their envelopes, and her ivory paper knife and the case for her glasses.

80

'She bade me take life easy, as the grass grows on the weirs . . .'

'Yes. You, my child, are young and foolish.'

'And you are full of tears?'

Aunt Mary stood up, the letters dangling from her hand. 'I am content. It's all I ever asked to be.'

Her next hours would be filled with getting the old man up and dressed. Clean. His breakfast inside him. Humouring him, soothing. Content or not, strain showed in the stretched lines of her face.

'You'll be in, won't you? Round the place. You'll keep an eye on him?'

Nancy nodded.

'You won't let him sit too long in the sun? It makes his head ache.'

'I know.'

'Of course you know, pet. I'm an old fusspot.'

She moved slowly towards the door. She moved always with grace, no slouching, her back straight without conscious effort. Old-fashioned, Nancy thought. I love her but I don't want to be like her. She paused in the doorway. 'You'll . . .?'

'Yes. I'll watch him like a hawk.'

'And there's raspberries to be picked. All, dear. don't just take the ones you can see.'

'I am the world's greatest raspberry picker.'

'I should be back by about half past six. You'll make sure he eats some lunch, won't you?'

'I'll shovel it into him.'

Nancy picked up the *Irish Times*.

Two civilians shot near Navan. Burning of military stores in Carrick on Shannon. Discharged prisoner shot by roadside near Limerick. Military activity in Dublin, many persons arrested. Well known journalist shot by sentry. Fighting resumes in Armenia. Shocking Galway crime. Lady Walsingham has left London for the Riviera. Lord and Lady Kilmaine, who spent last week in Dublin, have arrived in London. Arrivals at Kingstown per Royal Mail steamers include . . . She dropped the paper on the floor. Written there in black and white it all seemed meaningless.

I should have been a seagull, she thought, watching it all from the clearness of the air. Then I could have remained indifferent with impunity. There would have been no demands. She thought of flying on the wind, watching the houses creeping out pitilessly over the green fields, the smoke from the burnt-out buildings, the bodies uselessly crumpled by the roadside, the Royal Mail vessels back and forth, winter and summer on the grey, black, blue-green moving sea, and the gulls floating on its swell as they float on the air.

'Are you sitting there all day?'

Bridie banged a tray down on the sideboard.

'You gave me a fright. I was just thinking.'

'You'd do better to be out picking the raspberries before it rains.'

'It's a gorgeous day. It's not going to rain.'

'Fine before seven, rain before eleven,' said Bridie with morose conviction. 'Were you eating bread in my kitchen last night?'

'I was.'

'Crumbs.' The single word was a small explosion of severity.

'I thought I'd cleared it all up.'

'Didn't you get enough to eat below?' She began to pile plates on to the tray.

'I didn't stay. It was awful, I ran out on them. I went for a walk on the beach.'

'What did you do a thing like that for?'

'Impulse.'

Bridie gave a little snort of laughter.

'Impulse? If your aunt and I had had the impulse when you were little to give you the odd rat-tat on your backside, you wouldn't be impulsing round the place now. What did they think of you at all?'

'I don't know and I don't care.'

'You,' said Bridie, crashing the coffee pot down on to the tray, 'are supposed to be a lady. You were rared to be a lady.'

'Lady? After all, what's a lady?'

'You know well what I mean, and them Caseys is only

fit to be sweeping the streets, and you go letting your aunt down in front of people like that.'

'Women and men there are.'

'That's maybe the way you look at it, but there's more to all these things than meets the eye, and don't you go upsetting Her, She has enough to worry about as it is.'

Bridie always referred to Aunt Mary as Her, unless they were face to face, when a slightly grudging 'Mam' slipped through her lips.

'The punnets are on the kitchen table.'

'Thanks,' said Nancy.

Bridie picked up a small brush and pan from the sideboard and began to brush the crumbs from the table. As she leaned forward, her arms outstretched, she creaked, like her own wicker chair in the kitchen. Under her arms her dark blue dress had faded almost to white. She smelt eternally of the small white peppermints that she crunched between her remaining teeth throughout the day.

'Dreaming gets you nowhere.'

'I suppose not.'

Nancy got up and went to pick raspberries.

The day crawled gently along. Bridie had been right, and the rain had started spotting the garden path as Nancy was coming back with the raspberries. By twelve a grey mist of rain covered everything. Aunt Mary had driven off wrapped in a long brown macintosh and a soft leather hat with a brim that flopped around her face. It gave her the look of a leprechaun tired by too much cobbling. She continued to wave her hand through the window of the car until she had passed behind the trees at the bottom of the avenue.

'You can't see anything.'

The old man's petulant voice made Nancy jump. It was the first remark he had made to anyone since Aunt Mary had waved her way down the avenue. He had been established in his chair by the window, the plaid rug tucked round his legs, his glasses and his panama hat on the table beside him. He had dozed and mumbled meaningless words to himself, and from time to time had lifted the glasses to his eyes to scan the line. Occasional snatches of song had sent him to sleep again.

'There is nothing to see, Grandfather. Only rain.'

She got up from the sofa where she had been lying, reading a book. She went across the room and stood beside him. His white, very fine hair was stretched tight across the top of his head. The fingers clamped around the glasses looked already dead.

'There's never anything to see, Grandfather, only the field and the railway line.'

'I see things. I pass my day seeing things. These are very good glasses. Exceptionally so. German field glasses. Military issue.'

He looked down at the glasses with a certain pride.

'Loot.'

She squatted on the floor beside him and they both stared in silence for a moment at the rain-flecked window.

'Grandfather,' she said finally. 'Do you remember Robert? . . . well . . . Robert?'

'I just took them from this fellow who was lying in this gun emplacement. He was dead. Yes. A blooming Dutch fellow. Loot, I suppose you'd call it. It was frowned upon. A bad example and all that. I remember his face as if it was yesterday. Odd that. He had quite a decent face. Bloody savages those Dutch. After all, if I hadn't taken them, someone else would have.' There was a long pause. 'Wouldn't they?'

'I suppose so.'

'It was frowned upon. But everyone did it. You didn't make a song and dance about it, that was all.'

'Robert,' she suggested.

'I don't remember. It is very easy to confuse things.'

'If you can remember the face of a dead Boer, surely you can remember Robert.'

'If you kill someone, they tend to leave their face with you. As a sort of present.'

'You mean you killed the man whose glasses you took?'

'I suppose I had to. I don't remember the exact circumstances. I was after all a soldier. I remember saying to the young chap who was with me, he looks quite a nice fellow.

84

I remember that.'

'What did he say?'

'Yes sir, perhaps. Or nothing. There wasn't much he could say.'

'I suppose not.'

'Someone once said "Death is an old jest, but it comes to everyone".' He sighed. 'Kipling perhaps. Was it Kipling? It's the sort of thing Kipling would say.' Wearily he lifted the glasses to his eyes. 'It is impossible to see.'

'Turgenev. He said it. Turgenev.'

He didn't seem to hear or care.

'I never cared for the Russians,' he surprised her by saying after a long time of searching the line and field below it, and the grey disintegrating sky. 'Robert was a Bolshevist.'

'Oh Grandfather, surely not!'

'Or an anarchist or a socialist. Something infernal like that. I said to him once, I suppose you'll murder us all in our beds one night. I said something like that. Didn't take a feather out of him. His teeth were stained with tobacco.' There was a sudden scurry of wind and the trees waved their branches bravely. 'You only noticed it when he laughed. Brown streaks. I suppose it was tobacco.'

The effort of having spoken for so long seemed to have exhausted him. His head drooped, his fingers loosened their grip on the glasses and they fell to the floor. Nancy picked them up. The man on the beach, Cassius, didn't have brown streaks on his teeth. She was sure of that. Gently she put the glasses on his knee. His fingers groped for them. She crouched beside him listening to his faint breathing. What would she do if he died on her? Just like that, sitting in his chair? Stopped breathing? Total silence would fill the room and then she would know. Her heart jumped into her throat at the thought of it. Aunt Mary would come home gaily from the races and find them there in the silence. She put out a hand and touched his arm.

'Ah!' was all he said. He lifted the glasses. 'The last rose of summer left . . .'

'Oh Grandfather!' she muttered angrily, and went back to her book.

The rain eased off during the afternoon. The sun came

85

out eventually and cast black shadows over the flowerbeds and lawn.

The bell rang.

Someone pulled the brass handle by the hall door and the bell danced on its spring high up on the kitchen wall.

'Now who would that be?'

Bridie looked up at the bell over the top of the paper she was reading.

Nancy was at the bread and jam again. It was as if she knew that never in her life would bread and jam be so good again.

The bell jangled again.

'Whoever it is hasn't much patience.' Bridie rattled the paper up in front of her face again. Her chair creaked around her comfortably. 'You've got young legs.'

'Oh blow!' said Nancy, shoving the last bite into her mouth. 'It's bound to be someone awful, or nuns.'

Normally the only people who bothered to use the bell were those collecting for some charity or other; almost everyone else just opened the door and yoo-hooed their way into the house.

It was Maeve.

'Oh hello.' Nancy blushed. 'It's you.'

'The rain stopped and I felt like a little walk, so . . .' The ends of the yellow scarf tied round her hair moved gracefully in the wind. 'I just thought I'd come up and see if you were all right. Had recovered.'

'I just didn't feel well, all of a sudden. Sick . . . a bit dizzy . . . I didn't want to make a fuss . . . so I . . .' As she gabbled out the lies, her finger picked a little knob of paint on the door jamb.

'Did you go home to bed?'

'Fresh air . . . you know how sometimes what you really need is fresh air. I walked a bit. Anyway I do apologise. Will you come in?'

Maeve hesitated.

'Or we could sit in the garden. It always smells so nice after rain.'

'I can't stay long. I have to go up to town.'

Meeting Harry no doubt. Pink lampshades. Wine.

86

Bangles clinking across the table as they held hands.

'Have you had tea?'

'I never say no to a cup of tea. If it's not too much trouble.'

'No, no,' muttered Nancy vaguely. 'You go on round the back. You'll find deckchairs on the terrace. I'll be with you in a minute.'

She ran down the passage to the kitchen.

'Any tea left in the pot?'

Bridie remained behind the paper.

'Who's wanting tea?'

'Blooming old Maeve Casey. I never say no to a cup of tea.'

'You'd better make some fresh.'

'I'll just put some more water in the pot.'

Bridie dropped the paper on the floor.

Four killed in ambush.

'Make the girl a cup of tea and don't have her saying she got nothing but stewed tea in this house. And there's cake in the tin, if you haven't eaten it all when my back was turned.'

'Fuss, fuss, fuss. You'd think she was the Queen of England.'

Nancy emptied the clogged tea leaves into the sink and rinsed the pot out with boiling water.

'Let's hope no English Queen, nor King neither ever passes this threshold.'

'Don't be silly, Bridie, you know perfectly well if they ever came to Dublin, you'd rush up in your best clothes to cheer at them.'

Sniff.

'I wouldn't. I'm a republican.'

'You and your big words. Hurry up with that tea or Mademoiselle from Armentières will have gone home.'

Bridie pulled a magazine from under her behind and began turning the pages with her first finger and thumb.

'Don't forget the sugar.'

'Why don't you read proper books instead of those old lavatory paper magazines?'

'You write a book as good as one of these and I'll read it.

There's very good stories in this. True stories. And knitting.'

'Maybe I will.' Nancy put two cups on the tray. 'And I'll put you in it. The true story of Bridie Ryan.'

'That'll give the world a laugh.'

The two girls sat on slightly damp deckchairs, one on each side of a wrought iron table. Maeve refused a piece of cake. She put two lumps of sugar into her tea and in spite of the kitchen teapot and cups, her little finger crooked elegantly as she drank. The scent from Aunt Mary's rose-beds was everywhere. The drawing-room window had been opened and the weary voice of the old man sounded inter-mittently.

'Swift to its close ebbs out life's little day . . '

'Does he do that all the time?'

'He's old.'

'I know . . . but sing like that? All the time?'

'We hardly notice it.' Some obscure loyalty made her lie.

'How gorgeous the garden is looking! How many gardeners have you?'

'Well, we have Jimmy . . .' She tried to make it sound as if he were the first of a long line of gardeners. This is Jimmy, our head gardener.

'Jimmy?'

'He's getting on a bit now. He's been here since he was fourteen. His father used to look after the horses . . . years ago that would have been. Jimmy never does what he's told, but he's sweet. As Bridie says, he has his little ways. I don't know what we'd do without him.'

'Just Jimmy?'

'Aunt Mary gardens. She likes it. She knows the names and habits of all the flowers and trees. I always find that amazing. She can cut little bits off things and stick them in the ground and they'll grow.'

Maeve wasn't listening.

'Hold Thou Thy cross before my closing eyes . . .'

'It must be a lot of hard work for her. And she's not getting any younger.'

'She's not old.' Nancy spoke sharply. She thought of her aunt's weathered face and how, when she was tired, her eyes paled to an almost washed colour, losing for a while their brightness, their challenging look. 'Not nearly old.'

Maeve put her teacup down on the table and laced her hands behind her head, leaning back in the damp deckchair, preening herself slightly as she looked down the slope towards the roses. Yellow, red, pink, the ground beneath the bushes was littered with a patchwork of colours.

'I presume your aunt has told you . . .' her voice was casual, as if she were discussing the price of shoes, 'that my father is negotiating with her . . . with her . . . to buy this place. I suppose you know.'

Bewildered, Nancy looked at her in silence.

'. . . its glories pass away . . .'

'Which place?' she asked after a long time.

'Here. Ardmore. This house, these . . .' She gestured towards the roses.

'Negotiating?'

'Yes. With your aunt. He wants the land for development. You must have been told surely?'

Nancy began to laugh. When in doubt, laugh.

'He always thinks up such great ideas. He thinks this is just the sort of place people will want to live in. More and more they're moving out of the city. You can understand that, with the trouble and everything. They'll need nice houses and gardens. Tennis courts, all that sort of thing. And there's the sea and the golf club, and it only takes half an hour in the train to get up to . . . Nice people. Professional people and business people . . . Why are you laughing?' Away across the field a man climbed up the embankment and began to walk along the line. Nancy stopped laughing and followed him with her eyes as she tried to collect her thoughts.

'I'm afraid I don't understand.'

The distant figure disappeared behind the trees.

'It'll be a great thing for everyone. Not just for him. I wouldn't like you to think . . . For you, everyone. He's a great man for ideas.'

'Oh Thou who changest not abide with me.'

'Sing. Yes, sing,' said Nancy.

'Pardon?'

'Sorry,' said Nancy. 'I don't know why I said that.'

'You see, he would build your aunt a bungalow, down at the bottom of the hill somewhere, near the village. No stairs, that sort of thing, make life easier for her as she . . . gets . . . on.'

She unlaced her hands and sat up straight in her chair. She traced an invisible pattern on her silk skirt. Her nails shone with careful polishing, and were neatly shaped, but short so as not to interfere with her piano playing. Over the rosebeds the swallows were playing their evening game, swooping and soaring, almost brushing the leaves with their quivering wings.

'This house . . .?' Nancy couldn't ask the question.

Maeve leant over and touched her knee.

'You needn't worry. We won't pull it down. It needs money spent on it, He'll do that all right. A house like this should be looked after.'

'Charles Dwyer Esquire, late of the County of Cork.'

'I didn't know you had relations in Cork. My father's sister is married and lives down there.'

'He left Cork in sixteen something and began to build the house . . . I mean, it's not like it was then, lots of people have fiddled around with it since. He just came into my mind. Aunt Mary's the last Dwyer left . . . apart from Grandfather.'

'No one to carry it on?'

'No.'

'So you see . . . it's no great tragedy. Is it?'

'No great tragedy.'

The orange cat walked carefully along the wall and sat down with his back to them, his sleepy orange eyes watching the movements of the swallows.

'Does Harry know all this?'

Maeve got up from the chair.

'Would you look at the time. I must fly. I have to change. Thanks a million for the cup of tea. Don't move. I'll just cut across the field.' She stood looking down at Nancy. 'I'm glad you weren't . . .'

'It was just a passing dizziness. Thanks for calling.'

'You must come over soon. You and your aunt. We'd like

that. I'd really like to get to know you better.'

'Thank you . . .'

'Tooraloo.'

Maeve moved away. Down the steps and along the winding path through the roses, the yellow scarf lifting gently as she moved. At the gate into the field she turned and waved. Nancy didn't wave back.

'Why didn't you tell me before? Why on earth?'

They were sitting in front of the fire in the little study behind the drawing-room. The curtains were not pulled and they could see dim shadows of themselves against the black sky.

Aunt Mary had returned from the races gaily intoxicated by several wins, several drinks and the undemanding good humour of her friends. She had pushed the old man round the garden in his chair, talking animatedly, her eyes shining, her hands never still, punctuating sentences, describing, tweaking the dead heads from the roses, stroking lovingly, from time to time, the sleeve of his jacket. He presumably enjoyed the attentions, but never spoke, except at one moment to make some fretful remark, pointing as he spoke with a trembling finger, towards the railway line. After they had eaten their dinner, Aunt Mary wheeled him off and helped him to bed. Nancy sat by the fire and listened to the rising and falling of her voice and the little tremors of laughter that burst out from time to time. She loved the precise sounds of evening and night time, when every tiny noise had its own significance and clarity. At last her aunt had come into the room and closed the door.

'Tra la!'

She went over to the corner, where some bottles and glasses stood on a table, and poured herself a large whisky, and then, the energy draining away visibly from her face, taking with it the colour that had given it gaiety before, she sat down by the fire and leaned her head against the back of her chair.

'Why on earth!'

Aunt Mary frowned down into her now empty glass.

'Pet . . .'

She got up slowly and went and poured herself another drink.

'. . . I suppose I didn't want you to worry . . . brood perhaps over something . . . something about which you could do nothing.'

'You mean it's a *fait accompli*?' She wondered if they were already sitting in someone else's room.

'No . . .' Aunt Mary shook her head. 'I am still turning it over and over in my mind. Pringle is advising me. I always meant to tell you before anything . . .'

'What is he advising you?'

'Sense, dear. Mr Pringle is a very sensible man. I'm afraid the sensible thing to do is . . .'

'Is?'

'Sell. I'm afraid so.'

'It can't be.'

Aunt Mary smiled.

'It's really a question of making ends meet.'

There was a long silence.

'As bad as that?'

'I'm . . . well . . . it all boils down to five people, if you count Jimmy, and we have to count Jimmy really, all living off money that doesn't exist any longer. What comes in is far less than what goes out. Mr Pringle did explain it all. You see, since Gabriel was killed . . . I suppose we should have done something earlier.'

She took a drink from her glass and held the liquid in her mouth for a long time before letting it slide down her throat. Nancy watched the movement of her throat as she swallowed.

'It's been a little like those people pursued by wolves who throw everything out of the sledge until there's nothing left. I've kept going by selling little things. Silly, I admit. Now there's nothing left.' She sighed. 'I've never been much good at facing reality. Gabriel wouldn't have let this happen. He was practical and quick-witted. I've never been like that. Long ago there didn't seem the need . . . I suppose in a way we've been lucky to have things to sell. I don't even know about that. One ought to face reality. Really ought to.'

Nancy got up and went across to the window. She found

92

the darkness there oppressive; she couldn't bear their reflections another moment. She pulled the curtains.

'Perhaps if I'd thought about all this thirty years ago, or even twenty, I would have been able to cope ... make something credible ... not just drift. It'll be all right though. It's the people that matter, nothing else. Father and Bridie and poor old Jimmy. They'll be all right. And you're young. You will only notice a small irritation in your life. You won't mind for long because too many other things will be happening to you. You will be starting to live. Perhaps it will even prevent you from making a lot of similar silly mistakes.'

'Couldn't we keep the house?'

'We'll get a cottage somewhere. A nice old cottage.'

'Maeve said he'd build you a bungalow.'

Aunt Mary laughed.

'Don't be a bloody fool. We'll get a cottage up in the hills somewhere, looking over the sea, and that damn railway if possible. Father has to have something to look at with his blooming glasses. You can get digs in Dublin and come out and visit us at weekends.'

She had it all worked out.

'I only hope ...' she ran a finger around the rim of her glass and it sang, a long high-pitched note that took a long time to die ... 'they won't be too precipitate ... you know ... he will miss the trains ... and things. I wouldn't want him to be discomforted.' She smiled. 'Not discomforted at all. I suppose it would be best if he were just to ... I hate to think like that.'

'Is it very terrible being grown up?'

A burst of laughter.

'Pet, I wouldn't know. I don't think it's ever happened to me. Perhaps now.'

'You never answer important questions.'

'I try not to create confusion.'

'We could stay on though? Sell the rest and stay on ourselves.'

Aunt Mary shivered slightly and stretched out a hand towards the fire. 'No, no. I don't think it would work. It would just be another half-measure. Anyway I have enough

. . . Oh I don't know what you'd call it . . . foolish pride perhaps not to want to see the houses and the tennis courts squeezing up around us. Know that critical eyes were assessing us from behind white curtains, watching us pushing the dust under the carpets or only polishing the bottom halves of the windows. Maybe it's wrong to think like that but that's the way I am. Anyway this house is part of the deal. I suspect they want it for themselves.'

'Oh?'

'It's years since any money was spent on it. I'd like to see it receiving the attention it deserves. You'll be all right. I promise you that.'

The fire muttered and a slim blue flame quivered in the darkness in the back of the chimney.

'What can I do?' Nancy spoke suddenly after a long silence. 'I'd like to know if there was something I could do.'

'Oh no.' Aunt Mary's voice now was blurred with drink and tiredness. She giggled slightly, and then began to speak very rapidly, almost as if she didn't want Nancy to hear what she was saying. 'Yes. Of course. Yes. Everything's changing. You must realise that. I suppose it's for the best, but I don't imagine I will ever know for sure. Change takes time. You must be part of that. That's important. You must move, re-energise. Don't just drift as I have always done. Your grandfather's dead and I am dying. Not,' she held up a hand to stop Nancy speaking, 'that I have ever lived. I've been happy, calm and useless most of the time. The great thing to remember is that there is nothing to be afraid of. You learn that as you get older. We live in a state of perpetual fear. All the horrible things we do to each other, all our misunderstandings, are because of fear. All our terrible mistakes.' She giggled again. 'I think I must be terribly drunk.'

'A bit.'

'It doesn't matter one way or the other. Bridie'll be angry with me. She'll know when she brings me up my tea in the morning that I've had too much to drink and she'll click her tongue and give me the cold eye.'

'She'll hate a bungalow.'

'Cottage.'

'Cottage. She'll hate that too.'

'Not once she gets used to it. Cosy, easy, everything at hand. She won't know herself. She and I can spend our declining years sitting by the fire reading and playing cards. And that sinister cat.'

'It sounds dull.'

'Not at all. The world can go mad and we will sit and make our own quiet comments and back a few horses and sleep and remember things. Bridie and I have a lot of memories in common. I really must either go to bed or have another drink.'

The last standing piece of turf crumbled inwards on to the glowing ashes.

'Oh bed, I suppose,' said Nancy.

13 August

My dream would be that the wind should catch up this old house and whirl it away as it whirls the seagulls. It could land us gently on the edge of the sea somewhere with a racecourse in easy reach for Aunt Mary and a curving horizon of railway line alive with shining engines, goods trucks, carriages, points, signals, sidings, the whole lot, within nice range of grandfather's glasses. Nothing but pleasure for his last days, or years as the case may be. No anxiety, no sadness, just a miraculous happening. Silly dream. Still, like a child I have silly dreams. I can see them living here, a lovely pair, as Bridie will undoubtedly call them when the moment comes. He will keep the place up to the mark and she will play her white piano in the drawing-room and they will never notice our bruised ghosts lurking in the corners. I suppose in fact that their corners will be too clean and well lit for ghosts to be comfortable in. There will be nothing left of mother or Gabriel or the child who has sat for so many years on the top step of the terrace, not getting piles. There used to be horses in the stables and Uncle Gabriel hunted twice a week, and there was a boy who kept the tack, polished the lovely shiny boots. There was a smell of saddle soap and horse dung. The saddles are flaking now, out in the damp tack room. The little fire in the corner is never lit and birds drop twigs down the empty chimney and they fall out from the fireplace and litter the floor. Sometimes though you can still hear the sound of a horse backing up on the cobbles, the stutter of hooves, a soft whinny. If you're in the right mood of course. I was always afraid. I remember the thud my heart used to give when one of them would raise its head and move towards me. Martin was the boy's name. He used to whistle between his teeth as he rubbed and rubbed, curry-combed and polished their gleaming coats. He would lean his head against their warm necks and kiss them with the side of his whistling mouth. He's in prison in England now. He was caught after a raid on a barracks down near Cork somewhere. He was wounded, I think, and couldn't get away. Something like that.

They will make a lovely couple. I don't suppose he would ever love someone like me, even if I were five years older. She is so new and perfect and polished looking, and she won't be really kind to him and he'll probably never notice. They will both accept most graciously what the world has to offer. That's no crime. It's more of a crime I suppose to want to mess things up a bit. Oh God, don't let me be too feeble and please help me to stop biting my nails! Amen.

The wind got up again during the night, and in the morning the garden was littered with branches and whirling leaves. Nancy saw in her mind the beach strewn with wrack and driftwood. I'll light a fire, she thought.

'It's a lovely walking day,' she said. 'I think I'll go for a long long walk. I'll bring some fruit. I won't come back for lunch.'

'Mmm!'

'I don't think it'll rain, do you?'

'Mmm!'

'You could really stride for miles on a day like this.'

Aunt Mary never stirred from behind the paper. 'Tell Bridie before you go.'

She lit her fire about half a mile on the town side of the hut, halfway between the nuns' bathing box and the point. She had brought two newspapers and a box of matches as well as two bananas and an apple. She crumbled the paper page by page – crumpled the 'Fashionable Intelligence', the sports pages and the advertisements for White's Wafer Oatmeal and J. W. Elvery and Co. Ltd. ladies' and gentlemen's waterproof and rainproof coats, Robt. Roberts' pure China tea, and a one week sale of Clery's boots and shoes, the stock exchange reports and the Parliamentary reports and the news. She piled a pyramid of grey driftwood over the whole lot and put a match to it. The fire caught at once, and she sat watching the smoke curling up into the wind and wondered if grandfather were watching it through his glasses and whether a new set of memories curled into his mind with the smoke. She ate her bananas eventually as the fire died down into a pile of simmering ashes, and then she walked along the sea's edge towards the hut. She became aware suddenly that she was walking along beside someone's footmarks. Male shoe marks. The heels sank quite deeply into the sand and the soles were criss-cross patterned. She stopped walking and looked back along the beach. The marks came down from the railway line. Straight and purposeful they marched along the sand. No dog gallivanted beside them. Just a man on his own had walked that way. They moved up to the right and finally disappeared among the blocks of stone. Quite disappeared. She searched around carefully for any signs of them but found none. As she stood up straight again, she saw the man, Cass, watching her from beside a rock.

'Lost something?'

'Those aren't your footmarks?' She pointed back along the beach. 'You don't wear shoes like that.'

'Bravo, Sherlock Holmes!'

She blushed.

'There's been someone here?'

He nodded.

'Is there . . . is there . . .?'

She looked around.

'No. Come. It's cold here. Let's go indoors.'

They walked towards the hut in silence.

'You're cross?' he said as they arrived. He opened the door and held it for her.

'Let's go in out of the wind.'

'It's so careless. He left footmarks. Right the way along the beach.'

'There are no footmarks here.'

'A man. I didn't say you could have visitors. I don't like millions of people coming here to my . . .'

He stood looking at her for a moment and then sat down with his back against the wall. He took a bottle from his pocket and pulled out the cork. 'It was a messenger. That's all. He didn't come here. We met out there among the rocks. I have been waiting for him. He brought me a word or two of importance and some whisky. Have some and don't be cross.'

He held the bottle out towards her.

She shook her head.

'The last time I drank your whisky it had a horrid effect on me. Anyway young ladies of my age are not supposed to drink whisky.'

He laughed. He reached up to the shelf above his head and took down a mug. Carefully he poured a small amount from the bottle and held the mug out towards her.

'Here, even the most ladylike of young ladies could safely sip at that.'

She took the mug.

'I'm sorry if I was cross.'

'Come and sit down. I presume it was you in the distance, sending up smoke signals?'

'I love bonfires. Aunt Mary says the smoke kills you.'

'I think it would take a superabundance of bonfire smoke to kill you. Go ahead, taste it. Tell me if you like it.'

He drank some himself out of the bottle.

She took a cautious sip.

'It's good. It's not a bit like the last lot.'

'It's very special. It's not every day you get whisky like that. Only when a messenger of the gods arrives.'

'Messengers of the gods don't leave huge great footsteps on the sand. Does it have a special name?'

'It's a Scottish malt. Better than anything else in the world to drink. When you lead the sort of life I do. Somewhat peripatetic. If you lead a rather more stationary life, claret . . . a good old claret . . . takes a lot of beating.'

She laughed. 'You are a funny man.'

'I haven't spent my entire life eating bananas out of paper bags, you know.'

'I bet Grandfather saw your messenger coming along the tracks, you know. He doesn't miss much. He keeps telling us about the people he sees, but no one pays any attention to him. He rambles on, sometimes talking nonsense, sometimes not, only we never really bother to sort it out. Do you have elderly relations?'

'My dear Nancy, I jettisoned all family ties many, many years ago. I like to travel unencumbered.'

'Don't you get lonely?'

He shook his head and then took another careful drink from the bottle. He screwed the top on and put it down beside him on the floor.

'At the present time there is no space in my life for such an emotion. Maybe when I become useless . . . who knows . . . maybe then I will become lonely. The seagull on the roof isn't lonely. His eyes are like stones.'

'When you get useless, you can always sit in a chair and think about all the people you've killed.'

'My dear young lady . . .'

'I'm sorry. I really didn't mean to say that.'

'Of course you did. I feel no guilt about what I do, the way I think, so don't think you can appeal to what you might consider to be my better nature. There are conscience-less men, utterly unscrupulous, who will go to any lengths to make sure that the world remains the way they want it to remain. No possibility of change. They crush and destroy . . . aspirations . . . hope. People must at least be allowed to hope.'

'It's the killing . . .'

'After all,' he said gently, 'your grandfather was a killer too, and no one makes sarcastic remarks at him for that. Not at all. They gave him medals and a pension. He wasn't even killing to defend his own fatherland, indeed the very opposite. He was taking other people's land away from them. Creating an Empire for a little old lady with a thing like a tea cosy on her head. Indeed, had he been a younger man, he would probably be here, down the road somewhere, killing his fellow countrymen, destroying their dream. And yet . . .'

'Oh dear . . . oh no . . . !'

'. . . and yet he is a lovable, irritating old man who mumbles and sings and will probably die as every man should, in his own bed, and some people will cry.'

'I get very confused. Is that despicable?'

He leant back against the wall and began to laugh. As she watched him, she wondered if his own confusion were not almost as great as hers. The blind would always be leading the blind.

'I'm sorry to laugh,' he said eventually. 'There is absolutely nothing despicable about you. Believe that.'

'Aunt Mary's going to sell the house.'

'Oh!'

She watched his face carefully. The smile slowly left his mouth and his eyes brooded back into the past, seeing groves, paths, sunlight patterning the drawing-room carpet, the blooming of polished wood. Old days, old faces. His fingers fiddled for a moment, uncertainly, with the top of the bottle. 'Yes. I suppose it had to be like that, sooner or later. You would have had to do it anyway.'

'I don't think I would have thought of it as a possibility. Aunt Mary's much more practical than I am.'

'Who . . . ?'

'Houses,' she said. 'Lots of houses. Posh houses. It's . . . it's, well, close to the city really. The train . . .'

'So, my dear, you too will have a chance to travel without encumbrances.'

'I'd rather not.'

He finally unscrewed the top of the bottle and tilted a drink into his mouth.

'Coward!'

'No, I'm not. I just would have wanted to keep things on . . .'

'Coward!'

'Yes. I am.'

A wave crashed suddenly on the beach outside.

'The wind is getting up.' She couldn't think of anything else to say.

'I thought the hut might blow away last night. The seagull and I would have been transported to Never Never Land.'

'I wanted your sympathy.'

'Well you won't get it. Everything has to keep changing. It's a myth that the things of value get lost with change. That's not true. Next year will always be a better year than the year before last. You have the whole bloody world waiting for you. Someone has just lifted what could only be an appalling liability from your shoulders and you want sympathy. Oh God!'

'I love it here.'

'You just don't know any alternative. The sea is cold, the beach is stony, the east wind blows all through the winter. The sooner you get out of it the better. Your nest. Your sensible aunt is throwing you out, like some birds do with their young. Out and either fly or fall. You make me feel very old. I barely remember what it was like to be eighteen. I hunted at least twice a week, and didn't dare speak to the pretty girls I met at parties in the evenings. Your aunt being one of them.'

'Was she a pretty girl?'

'Very, but a little sharp if I remember correctly. And you must stop biting your nails. It's a beastly habit. Think what happened to the Venus de Milo.'

She blushed and curled her fingers into the palms of her hands. 'Oh, that's mean!'

'Not at all. It's only what any self-respecting father would say to his daughter.'

'Have you any children?'

He shook his head.

'No encumbrances. I had a wife once, but she didn't really like me very much when she got to know me. That was all in my younger days.'

'Why didn't she like you?'

'Curiosity killed the cat.'

'Well?'

'I suppose when I married her, I was a someone. I could have told you my name and address. In fact I used to carry little cards round in my pocket and leave them around for people so that they would know I existed. She liked that. I had a house in London. She liked that too. A recognisable position, fairly well up at the top of the heap. She had been brought up to expect all sorts of lovely things to keep happening to her. She moved on to someone who was able to give her a better life than I could have. After five years of marriage I had merely become an embarrassment to her.'

'Was she beautiful?'

'Yes, I suppose so. She had a beautiful face and body.'

'That's important, isn't it?'

He smiled slightly at the anxiety in her face.

'Just another sort of encumberance. A woman can spend years of her life staring at other women and wondering if they're more beautiful than she is. Years staring at herself in the glass, touching the skin below her eyes with anxious fingers. I used to watch her. I thought, to begin with, it was most lovable . . . then . . .' He shrugged slightly. 'Just another liability.'

'I wonder,' was all Nancy said.

She stood up. He watched her carefully as she unfolded herself from her rather crouched position on the floor. Her limbs as well as her mind were troubled by the approach of adulthood. She moved them from time to time with sombre grace and then, as if aware of the charm that this might have, she seemed deliberately to destroy any false impression she might be making by some crude and clumsy gesture. He was alarmed to find that he was touched by her inexpertise. He took another quick drink from the bottle. The damn stuff, so necessary to him, wouldn't last long if he went on like this. She stood looking down at him. As always, when she was with him, she was disturbed by how deathly tired he looked.

'Will there be more messengers coming?' she asked.

'No. He will be the only one. Quite soon I will be going. I have been waiting for him to come.'

'I don't know whether to take you seriously or not.'

'I take you seriously.'

'Oh shut up!'

She pushed the door open. The sand and little stones were blowing in savage little gusts just above ground level and then settling for a moment before being whirled on again along the beach.

'Is there anything you want?'

She spoke with her back to him, staring at the sea.

'Do you ever go into town?'

'I can.'

She turned and looked at him. The hut seemed very dark, his figure almost like a ghost, sitting quite still, one knee bent. Only his eyes glittered with life.

'If I were to ask you to do a message for me . . . ?'

The afternoon train from Wicklow came round the bend and lurched past on the track above them. Smoke and sparks were tossed inland over the fields. She hoped that Grandfather was awake to see it.

'Yes,' she said, when the noise of the train had passed on down the line. 'I'd do a message.'

'You're sure?'

'Yes.'

'I'll meet you on the railway line tommorrow morning. Up near the bridge. Ten o'clock.'

'I can come here . . .'

'Near the bridge.'

'All right.'

'Thank you. You don't have to worry.'

'No.'

She flapped a hand awkwardly at him.

'Well . . .'

'Goodbye, Nancy.'

'Goodbye.'

She closed him into the darkness and climbed up on to the line. Sparks settled on the grass, the smoke still hung above the trees.

The two Miss Brabazons had been having tea with Aunt Mary and were just on the point of leaving as Nancy came up the avenue.

'Hail,' shouted the tall Miss Brabazon, waving a hand furiously above her head.

The small Miss Brabazon, who was very small, put out her hand to be shaken.

Nancy shook it.

'Good afternoon.'

'We've just come back from Marseilles. We thought we'd

drop over and tell Mary that we were safely returned. She never thought she'd see us again.'

'Near Marseilles. Not actually Marseilles. It's a smelly brute of a place.'

The tall Miss Brabazon moved over to their Daimler and began to pat its bonnet as if it were a horse.

'Which is why we're so brown.' The small Miss Brabazon pushed one of her sleeves up and held her arm out for Nancy to inspect.

'Marvellous!' said Nancy.

'The Camargue. Bullfights and all that. Frightfully exciting. And there was this amazing hot wind. Hot. Golly!'

Nancy wondered if she were about to offer the car an apple.

'And dear old car behaved like a perfect gentleman. Didn't he, George?'

The small Miss Brabazon nodded.

'Next time Mary must come. You really must, Mary. It was perfectly safe. We told you it would be perfectly safe.'

'We'll see,' said Aunt Mary.

'He never even flinched at French petrol.' She gave the car a final pat and looked Nancy up and down.

'You've grown.'

'Of course she's grown,' said her sister. 'It's the age for growing.'

'Nonsense, some people stop growing when they're thirteen. You're as tall as Mary.'

'Celia is obsessed with people's heights.'

'Your mother wasn't tall . . .'

'In France they thought she was *un monsieur Anglais* . . . They screamed when they found out that she was really a woman.'

' . . . she was knee high to a bee, in fact. Your father was tall. A really tall man. Perhaps you're taking after him.'

'Tum, tiddle um tum!' The small Miss Brabazon danced towards the car.

'You must tell Nancy all about your adventures some time,' said Aunt Mary.

'And the dear old general.'

'Yes.'

'The old pet. I'm so sorry we weren't able to see him today.'

'Visitors fuss him a little at the moment.'

'We'll come and have dinner. How about that?'

'That would be lovely.'

'Saturday after the races?'

'Perfect.'

The tall Miss Brabazon leaned across the bonnet.

'My dear . . . Do get in, George, and stop fidgeting round like that . . . did we tell you about the Shinners the other night trying to pinch the car?'

Aunt Mary looked alarmed.

'My dear Celia . . .'

'There we were all dressed up on our way to dinner at the Pilkingtons', the night after we got back from France . . . just driving along the back road to Roundwood. They'd pushed this cart across the road so we had to stop and then they jumped out of the ditch at us waving guns . . .'

'I screamed,' said George complacently.

'What did you do?'

'They had those scarves draped all over their faces and one of them said . . . I must say, very politely . . . "I beg your pardon, Miss, but we want your car" . . .'

'Imagine,' said George.

'My dear, I just put out my hand and pulled down the scarf and who was it but Tommy Roche from our back cottages. If you lay one finger on this car, This Car, I said, I'll tell your mother what you're up to when she's not looking and she'll tan your rebel backside for you.'

Aunt Mary laughed.

'Honestly, Celia, you have a nerve! What happened?'

'And get that cart out of the way, I said. We're late for dinner already.'

'And they did,' said George. 'Imagine.'

'Thank you, I said, very politely. Any other car . . . any other . . . the Morris for instance . . . but not This Car. You should know perfectly well. After all, he's a sort of a household pet. "I'm sorry, Miss," said Tommy, "we thought youse was still in France." So we drove on. I never heard if they got a car or not, or what they wanted it for.

Something terribly nefarious, I'm sure.'

'Wasn't that a scream?'

'Did you go to the police?'

'Don't be silly, Mary dear. They might have got into trouble.'

She gave the car a final loving rub and jumped into the driving seat.

'We'll call for you on Saturday. We'll go in this car. I was crippled after the last time we went to the Curragh in yours.'

She pulled on her gloves, smoothing the wrinkles out of each finger with care.

'It's your long legs, rather than Mary's car, you have to blame for that.'

'Rubbish!'

She pressed the starter button and the car began to vibrate.

'Ah! Good old fellow.'

She put her head out of the window and spoke in as low a voice as she could manage.

'Whatever you do, Mary dear, don't worry. Everything is going to be all right. We'll have dinner on Saturday; don't forget to tell Bridie. Goodbye, Nancy, look after your aunt.'

She put a hand on the horn, which snarled gently, more like a tiger than a horse, Nancy thought, then they were off in a flurry of gravel and smoke.

'Phew!' said Nancy.

'She drives that thing as if it were a stage coach.' Aunt Mary still waved her hand after her friends. 'I've told them about . . .'

'Mmmm!'

'After all, I've known them all my life.'

'I can't imagine them ever being children.'

'So I thought I should tell them . . .'

They went into the house. Grandfather's voice, singing softly, reached them as they entered the hall. Nancy wondered how tall her father really was.

'. . . I'd have told them before except they were away. Asked their . . . think they have a little house for us. Isn't that splendid. Over near Laragh. No one's been in it for several years so it needs a lot of work done on it.'

'I think I'll go up to town tomorrow afternoon. Can I do any messages for you?'

'I really shuddered at the thought of all that searching. Of course we won't have the sea, but I expect we'll get used to that . . .'

'Mary, is that you?'

'I'll go up on the two o'clock train.'

'Yes, pet, I'm just coming . . . or railway either, but he'll just have to find something else to look at. Bridie has cousins over that way. It sounds . . .'

'Mary!'

'. . . ideal. Don't you think?'

'Yes. Anything in town?'

'Perhaps library books, dear. Coming Father. Coming this minute.'

She disappeared into the drawing-room.

Nancy ran upstairs to her bedroom and looked out of the window. She saw below her the sloping fields scattered with neat houses, flowerbeds, rose pergolas, rockeries, here and there a fanciful summerhouse; washing floated on discreetly hidden lines, motor cars were parked on gravel sweeps, and high hedges, neatly trimmed, not a twig out of place, kept the neighbours safely insulated from each other. There would have to be tennis courts, too, she thought, and kitchen gardens, and the sun would have to be ordered to shine permanently.

If my father is taller than the tall Miss Brabazon, he must be very tall indeed. A skyscraper of a man. Taller than Cassius on the beach. Taller than Harry.

'Yoo-hoo!'

Taller than Mr De Valera, of whom she had seen photographs, standing on various platforms head and shoulders above his companions.

'Yoo-hoo!'

A soft ball of earth hit the wall beside her and scattered on to the sill and her hands.

'Oh!'

'You look like Rapunzel leaning out of her window, only your hair's not long enough.'

Harry stood below on the path.

'Hello. I always thought that was a silly story anyway, because by the time her hair had grown that long she'd have been about a hundred. So would he. Far too old to be carrying on like that.'

'Magic. It was all magic. Now that you're back from whatever far-off dream you were in come and have a swim. I feel like a swim.'

'He'd have had to stand at the bottom of the tower weeping piteously about having wasted his life waiting for her hair to grow . . . Oh save me, God, from extreme old age!'

'Nancy, wake up. Will you or won't you swim?'

'Are you speaking to me?'

'Don't be an ass. Come and swim.'

'What about Maeve?'

'She's just had her hair done. I came down in the train with her.'

Nancy salmmed the window down.

Hair done, indeed! She pulled her bathing togs and her towel off the hook on the back of the door and ran down the stairs.

'I presumed you were coming.' His voice was peevish. At any moment, if she wasn't careful, he might stop speaking to her again.

She took his arm and marched him across the terrace and down the steps.

'I can never resist a swim. It's going to be freezing though. The wind is blowing straight in from the sea.'

'Darling.' Aunt Mary's voice called from the window.

Nancy waved her towel in the air.

'A very quick swim.'

'Don't be late for dinner. Hello, Harry.'

'Hello, Mary. I promise she won't be late. A quick dip. In and out. Straight out.'

'Don't stand about in your wet togs, dear. That's an east wind,'

'Fuss, fuss, fuss,' said Nancy. 'Don't do this, don't do that. I'm not an idiot.'

'You're not always very sensible.'

'Immature, you called me.'

'That's right.'

'Well, I'll tell you something. I'm not going to be im-mature for long. I've made up my mind. I think . . . well . . . first of all I'll lose my virginity, that's a terrible liability, and then I'll join the Republicans. What do you think of that for a plan?'

She looked at him out of the side of her eye. He looked angry.

'You need a good spanking.'

He unhooked himself from her arm and walked sternly on down the hill in front of her.

'Can't you take a joke? Or two?'

'I deplore bad taste. Particularly from a child like your-self. You don't know what you're talking about.'

'What's bad taste about either virginity or Republican-ism?'

'I don't know why I put up with you.'

She ran up beside him and put her arm through his again.

'I do. It's because I love you and you're secretly rather pleased and flattered. You love to see the admiration glow-ing from my eyes.'

'Rot!'

He began to laugh and squeezed her arm close in to his side.

'You're a terrible leg-puller, Nancy. I don't suppose I have much sense of humour. I've always been told I haven't.'

'Won't it be amazing when this field is covered with desirable residences?'

He didn't answer.

'We are probably at this moment striding,' she strode for a moment, 'across someone's precious rosebed, trampling the pink and yellow hybrid teas into the earth. Getting thorns into our legs. Or . . .' she let go of him and began to run, 'running through the dining room, where some startled maid is laying the table for dinner, polishing up the glasses with the corner of her apron. Oops, sorry!' She stopped dead in front of Harry. 'Close your eyes like a good chap, Madam has been discovered in her bath. Only a sponge to protect herself.' She climbed over the gate and out on to the road. Harry stood in the field and looked at her.

'Yes.' He said. He opened the gate and walked politely

through it and then closed it behind him.

'Maeve told me that she's told you.'

'Over there,' she pointed across the road to the stretch of field below the railway, 'the houses will be a little less superior because the smoke from the passing trains will be a nuisance to everyone. Smuts will float in through the open windows. Washing will get . . .'

'It's really a very good idea. Good for everyone.'

'Of course.'

'What you might call a godsend for Mary.'

'Absolutely.'

'I'm glad you're being sensible about it.'

'I am being amazingly sensible. How long have you known about it?'

Much to her amazement, he blushed slightly.

'Oh . . . a while.'

They reached the path under the arch. She bent down to take off her shoes. She was never able to bear sand in her shoes, rubbing and grinding away at the soles of her feet and getting in between her toes. Under the arch the sand was always cold and slightly damp. When it rained, the water dripped down through the cracks between the sleepers and it never seemed to dry away. A boy and a girl leaned against the stone wall of the arch whispering to each other. Far away along the beach a man threw a stick for two dogs; everyone else in the world had gone home. The wind was bitter. Nancy wriggled out of her clothes and into her togs. Harry already had his on under his trousers. He stood waiting for her, looking beautiful and serious, the sun making a halo round his head. She picked up his hand and kissed it.

'Come,' she said, starting to run towards the sea. 'This is probably the last bathe we will enjoy together. Tomorrow I'm thinking of starting on a life of crime. Maturing crime.'

He took a hold of his sense of humour and laughed.

'Ha hahaha!'

They ran together into the retreating sea.

A cloudless day.

At ten o'clock she went down to the railway bridge as he

had told her to. She watched him coming along the track with quick confident steps. He covered two sleepers with each stride, she noticed. As he came closer, she saw that he was wearing a tweed suit and a brown hat, which he took off and waved at her. He looked for all the world like a country gentleman out for some exercise, only he lacked the dog at his heels. In one hand he held a small attaché case.

'Good morning.' He put his hat back on his head again.

It was a bit like being in Grafton Street, she thought.

Down below them on the beach the horrid little Fenton children were throwing sand at each other, while their nanny read a book on a brown rug. He took an envelope out of his pocket and held it out to her. She took it and put it into her pocket without looking at it. That seemed the right thing to do. They stood looking at each other. It was odd to see him dressed like that.

He was wearing what looked very like a regimental tie. She wondered where he had kept his clothes over the last week, they looked so neat and cared for.

'I presume you know Bewley's Café in Grafton Street?'

'Bewley's Oriental Café,' she said somewhat idiotically. 'Yes.'

'You go through the shop into the café at the back.'

She nodded.

'Sit down at the first table on the right inside the door and give this envelope to the young man who will be there. He'll buy you a cup of coffee, or tea if you prefer.'

She wanted to ask what to do if there was no young man there, or if the table were full, but she presumed that all that had been taken care of.

'Have you got that?'

'First table on the right. Young man.'

'I am very grateful.'

He took off his hat once more and bowed slightly towards her.

'If you wouldn't mind walking on the beach for a few minutes. It would be a good idea.'

She slithered down through the rocks and stood on the sand watching him stride along the line towards the station.

When she could no longer see him, she took the envelope out of her pocket and looked at it. There was nothing written on it at all. Disappointing in a way.

She arrived home as Aunt Mary and her grandfather were having their morning coffee.

'I saw you,' said the old man, as she came into the room.

Her heart gave a little jump.

'Yes, darling. He says he saw you talking to a man on the railway line.'

'I just said good morning. That was all. It was just a man walking along.'

'I saw you,' said Grandfather, 'talking to a man.'

'Good morning was all I said, He . . . um . . . took off his hat.'

'You can't be too careful whom you talk to,' said Aunt Mary.

'He reminded me of someone,' said Grandfather.

Nancy felt herself go red.

'Don't be silly. He was only an old tramp. He couldn't possibly have reminded you of anyone.'

She went upstairs to change into her tidy clothes.

At the first table on the right a young man was reading a book. A cup of coffee steamed on the table. The book lay flat beside it. He leant his forehead on his hand. She pulled out the chair opposite to him and sat down. He continued reading. Perhaps she'd got it wrong, she thought. She looked cautiously around. People were eating cream cakes with tiny silver forks.

'Hello,' she said.

He looked across at her. His two top front teeth were rather large and came down over the outside of his lower lip as he smiled, giving him the look of a friendly rabbit.

'Hello.'

He closed the book and pulled it slightly towards him with a nervous gesture, as if he were afraid she might steal it. He had curly brown hair that he had tried without success to control with a dose of hair oil.

'Will you have a cup of coffee?'

'Thank you.'

'Or would you rather have tea?'

'Oh coffee. It always smells so good here. So delicious . . .'

He nodded brusquely and began to click his fingers for the waitress.

'Miss?'

Nancy opened her bag and felt in it for the letter. It was there all right. Safe. She held it lightly in her fingers inside the bag.

The waitress came over to them.

'Yes sir?'

'Two coffees, please. Would you like a cake or something?'

Nancy shook her head.

The girl went away, writing down their order on her little pad as she moved.

The young man ran a finger round the inside of his stiff collar. It was making a sore red mark on his neck. Nancy took the letter out of her bag and pushed it across the table to him. He took it quickly from her and put it, without looking at it, into the inside top pocket of his coat. He looked a little more relaxed.

'Thanks.'

She gave him a little nod and wondered if that were all they were going to say to each other. She envisaged fifteen minutes of silent coffee drinking, each of them trying to pretend the other wasn't there.

'What's your name?'

'Nancy Gulliver.'

The teeth came down again over the lower lip.

'I didn't know anyone was really called Gulliver. That's great. I've learned something today. My mother always says you should learn something new each day.' He shoved his hand across the table for her to shake. 'I'm Joe Mulhare. Howaya?'

She held his fingers for a moment. She noticed that he, to, savaged his nails.

'Are you still at school?'

She blushed and then scowled.

'Of course you're not.' He answered his own question quickly. 'You just look young . . . well youngish. Let's say

114

that.' He leaned towards her and grinned. 'Let's settle for youngish.'

'I'm eighteen,' she said severely. 'Only just though. It's a terrible thing to look young. Nobody takes you seriously.'

The waitress came back with two cups of coffee, which she placed on the table. That meant that he had two cups of coffee steaming in front of him.

'Thank you,' they both said simultaneously, then they laughed.

'That's a magic,' said Nancy. 'You can have a wish. We can both have a wish, but we mustn't tell . . .'

He held out his hand and she took it, and they both wished for a moment.

Nancy wished the same wish that she had wished for years, that Harry might one day love her, then for the first time she regretted having wasted a perfectly good wish on a lost cause. She wondered what Joe Mulhare had wished.

'How old are you?'

'I'm eighteen too.'

'Well honestly . . . !'

'I'm nearly nineteen. I've had a very full life. That's why I have that look of wisdom round my eyes.'

She burst out laughing. He fiddled with the book on the table and then picked it up and put it in his pocket.

'What are you reading?'

He looked a little embarrassed.

Hamlet.

Hamlet?

'Have you ever seen it?'

She shook her head. 'No. We read it at school. Round the class, you know, I was Claudius. I always get the horrid people to play. I must have an evil personality. Hamlet this pearl is thine; here's to thy health . . .'

She lifted her cup and toasted him.

'I'd give a lot to see that play. It's great stuff,' said Joe.

'What do you do? You know . . . work?'

'Well at the moment I'm fully occupied in reading *Hamlet* and fighting for freedom.'

'Don't be silly . . .'

'What do you mean, don't be silly! Isn't that enough for

115

anyone? I bet it's more than you're doing.'

'Well . . . yes . . . but . . .'

'But what?'

'Oh just but . . . How do you earn your living is what I meant?'

'I don't. I live on charity. I thought of going into the railways, but I didn't like the idea of spending the rest of my life punching tickets.'

'I thought all boys wanted to be engine drivers.'

He dropped two lumps of sugar into his second cup of coffee and watched the disturbance in the cup for a moment.

'Yeah,' he said. 'A lot of them do right enough. It doesn't appeal to me any more.'

He tasted the coffee. 'My father died in prison.'

'Oh! How awful! I'm sorry.'

'No need to be sorry. He was a good man. I see by your face that you don't realise that sometimes good people end up in prison.'

'I . . .'

'I don't know why I'm telling you, but I am.'

They both gulped at their coffee.

'He was a union man. He came from Belfast. That's a funny old place up there. A lot of union fellows came from there. They put him in prison during the lock-outs and . . . well . . . he died. He was never strong. I thought . . . as you asked me . . . when I got to thinking, that was . . . that I'd try and do something that he'd have liked me to do. Not just punching tickets. So . . . do you understand?'

'Well . . .'

'No,' he said gloomily. 'I don't suppose you do.'

He looked more like a rabbit than ever. She had a strong impulse to touch him. To stretch out her hand and stroke his arm. She picked up her spoon and stirred her coffee instead.

'Why should you?'

'I'd like to understand. Believe that.'

'You see, when people ask for rights and don't get them, then they have to fight. I think he would have understood that.'

'And supposing you don't get them even if you do fight?'

116

'You go on. There's always someone left to go on.'

'Oh dear! Yes. I suppose there is. Perhaps you'd be better off punching tickets.'

He grinned. 'That's what my mother says. Lookit, I'm sorry. I don't know what's got into me. I don't usually moan or groan.'

'It must be too much *Hamlet*.'

'Maybe. How come you're mixed up in all this anyway? Your sort usually keep their noses clean.'

'I'm just doing a kindness for a friend . . . more an acquaintance . . . perhaps that would be the right thing to call him.'

'Yes. An acquaintance. He doesn't allow himself friends.'

'Do you know him?'

'No. Not me. I just run messages too. They say he's English.'

'No. I don't think so.'

'He's not one of us anyway. One of the people.'

'Everybody's one of the people.'

'Ah no! That's not true. You know it's not true. There are some people who just see a lot of other people as animals. Nothing more than that, animals without minds or feelings. Use them, like animals, and throw them away when they become useless. Sick, old. There's dogs in this country treated better than a hell of a lot of the people. That's what my father used to say. I don't remember him very well, but I remember a lot of the things he said. I remember when they came to tell us he was dead. My mother cried . . . and cursed.'

'The people who put him in prison?'

'No. Him. She was up from the country and she could be very free with the curses. She stood in the middle of the room and screamed dreadful curses. She felt she'd been deserted. It was frightening at the time. It upset the neighbours.'

'What a strange thing to do!'

'She always felt he ought to leave things alone. Mind his own business. He had enough on his plate without taking on the world. Wasn't he lucky enough to have a job; he should thank God and get on with it. Not be making

117

enemies. She shouted it at him daily. I could never understand why they had to shout.'

'Perhaps he'd still be alive if he'd listened to her.'

'Perhaps, but I like him better the way he was.'

'Dead.'

'Even if he is dead. He's probably better off dead.' He
laughed. 'Forming the heavenly hosts into trades unions.
God, I can see him!'

'Better working conditions for cherubim and seraphim.'

'Shorter hours for archangels.'

He looked at her in silence.

'I like you. There's something about you. You're not one
of us but . . .'

'I . . .'

'You aren't. But you could be for us. That's what matters.
Drink up your coffee and we'll go for a ride on a tram.'

He clicked his fingers again for the waitress.

'Or maybe you don't like trams? Maybe you've got things
to do?'

She shook her head.

'I love trams. I have to catch the quarter to six train home
though.'

'Bill, miss.'

He was eating the sugar at the bottom of one of his cups
with his spoon.

'We'll go out to Dalkey on the tram and you can get
your train from there. We'll sit on the top and you can let
your hair blow over the side. It's great to meet a girl who
hasn't cut her hair off. They're all at it. Crowning glory, my
mother calls it. She nearly had a fit when my sister came in
with her hair up to her ears.'

'Did she curse her?'

He laughed.

'She saves her curses for catastrophes. If you use a curse
too often you sort of weaken its power.'

He took the bill from the waitress and winked at her.

'Go raibh maith agat.'

She drooped her eyes disapprovingly.

'None of your dirty talk in here.'

She walked away, offended.

He looked across at Nancy and laughed.

'There's a girl with a suspicious mind. All I said was thanks.'

'It was the look in your eye that gave her ideas.'

She gathered up her bag and the parcel of library books for Aunt Mary.

He had a cap, which he put on as they left the café. She wondered if it had holes for the ears that she felt must be pushing their way up through his disordered hair. He didn't bother to walk on her outside as Harry always did, making a point of always manoeuvring her to the inside of the pavement. Two small girls in bare feet held out their hands.

'Lady . . .'

She paused for a moment wondering if she had any coppers in her purse, but he pulled at her elbow.

'Come on.'

'Lady . . .'

One of the children, noticing her hesitation, ran a few steps after her.

'Lady . . .'

'Where's the point?' he said.

His arm was firmly through hers. He walked quite quickly, his head hunched down into his shoulders, perhaps to alleviate the discomfort of his stiff collar.

'One day there will be no beggars.'

'But now . . .'

'A couple of pennies from you doesn't help.'

A very tall policeman ordered them across the road with a wave of his white gloved hands. A young man in a motor hooted impatiently as the crowd rushed forward. Two huge horses pulling a dray shifted from foot to foot, their harness jingling as they moved. The drayman wore a sack over his head and hanging down his back. A lorry full of auxiliaries, ignoring the policeman, edged its way through the crowd. A tram came round the corner from College Green.

'Run,' said Joe.

They ran along the narrow pavement, Joe pulling her along by the hand, and clambered on to the platform of the tram.

'Nancy.'

Startled at hearing her name called, she nearly dropped the library books. She looked round. With a cackle from the overhead wires the tram lurched forward. Harry was standing on the pavement.

'Nancy . . .'

He took his hat off.

'Oh, hello.' She smiled as casually as possible.

'What on earth . . .!'

'Up, up, up.' Joe shoved her towards the stairs. The tram swayed. Harry stood, hat in hand. looking after them. They climbed the stairs and lurched forwards to the front seat. Above them the trolley sparked and crackled as they turned the corner into Nassau Street.

'What an unfortunate happening!'

She settled herself into the seat and Joe sat down beside her.

'That fellow?'

'He'll fuss. He'll ask all sorts of stupid questions. Who you are? Where were we going? Why this? Why that? He'll probably tell Aunt Mary.'

Below them in College Park they were playing cricket. A tall white figure ran, bat outstretched. There was a touch of turning colour in the heavy green of the trees.

'What'll you say?'

'I'll think of something.' She smiled. 'I'm jolly good at inventing things. I have to be. I lead a very sheltered life. All my movements are catalogued.'

'No harm, for a young one like you with not much sense.'

They smiled at each other.

The journey took the best part of an hour. The wind reddened their faces and once almost got away with Joe's cap; but he felt it lifting from his head and grabbed it in time.

In Kingstown the tram stopped for a ten-minute rest. Down the road to the left they could see the yatchts bobbing gently in the harbour. A couple of auxiliaries came up the stairs and walked along between the seats, looking casually at the passengers. Nancy tried not to think of the envelope in Joe's pocket. No one looked at the two men, their guns in their hands ready for using. No one spoke until they had climbed down again and stepped on to the road.

'I hope I haven't wasted your afternoon?' she said.

'I wouldn't say it has been wasted.' He smiled at her.

The driver got down from his platform and twitched at the rope that held the trolley in place. There were more sparks.

'Isn't it amazing,' she said. 'All those sparks that keep us rushing along. Wouldn't you like to drive a tram?'

'No. I'd prefer a train. I'd find all those same old streets depressing, and the crowds, and stopping all the time to let people on and off. An express train. Tearing through the countryside frightening the cows.'

'It shows how little you know about the country if you think that cows are frightened of trains. They don't mind them at all.'

'Well just tearing through the countryside, then, blowing my whistle, leaving everything else behind.'

The tram, rested, began to sway forward again along the narrow street.

'I don't suppose we'll ever meet again.' He spoke suddenly, his voice low.

'You never know.'

He took off his cap and looked inside it for a moment, as if the words he wanted to say were written in there.

'That's always one of the troubles with life. People get thrown about a lot. Here, there and everywhere. I'd like to meet you again.' He put the cap back on his head and looked at her. 'I don't mean tomorrow. Not now, in a while when . . .'

'When what?'

'When we know a little more. When . . .' He made a gesture with his hands.

'Yes. I'd like to as well.'

'Really?'

'Really.'

He smiled.

'Then it will happen again, so it will. Remember that.'

He took his cap off again and with a sudden gesture threw it over the side of the tram. It fell to the ground and blew into the gutter, avoiding the wheels of a bicycle.

'I hated it,' said Joe, 'Absolutely hated it.' He took her hand and held it.

'What'll your mother say?' She was laughing as she spoke.

'She'll give me one all right with her fist and then she'll go out and buy me another. She thinks I'll die of cold or consumption or something if I go around with a bare head.'

'She sounds a bit like Aunt Mary. You must be a real trial to her.'

'Yeah, I expect so. She hates to think I might end up like my father. She's a good woman though.'

'I'm sure she is.'

'So when I come up to you one day and say hello, Nancy, you'll remember me, won't you?'

'The boy, whatshisname, who threw his cap out of the tram. What is his name?'

'Anything. Just remember me.'

'Yes. I will.' She crossed her heart with her right forefinger. 'Cross my heart and hope to die.'

He looked surprised. 'You say that too?'

'Everyone says that,' she said with conviction.

'I've often thought I'd like to go to college. Get a bit of education into myself. Learn a lot of long words so I could dazzle people in the years to come.'

'You could just buy a dictionary.'

'You know . . . Nancy.' He squeezed her fingers. 'I'd like to write . . . that's what I'd really like to do . . . but I'm afrid of making a bloody eejit of myself.'

'I'd like to write too . . . but I'm afraid I'll never find anything to write about.'

'I've never met anyone else who wanted to write.'

'No more have I. Potential writers are thin on the ground. Particularly where I come from.'

They looked at each other, amazed.

'I have this sort of notebook where I write things down. A diary. Not exactly. I put things down so I won't forget. Forgetting is so easy.'

'Will you put down about me?'

She blushed.

'Well, it's a thought diary rather than a happening diary.

122

I'm getting a little fed up with it.'

'Just make a note of my name. I'd like to think of it written there in your book.'

She smiled.

'I remember when I was about ten I thought this boy was marvellous and I used to write his name on bits of paper, over and over again, and then tear them up and throw them in the fire. Did you ever do that sort of silly thing?'

'What was his name?'

She thought for a moment.

'Do you know, I honestly don't remember. I only met him once at tea with some friends.'

She burst out laughing.

'Isn't that silly? And I really thought he was the most wonderful boy in the world. I thought about him for months. Had great dreams.'

'You just make sure you write my name down and don't throw it in the fire.'

'We're nearly there,' she said abruptly.

'Yes.'

Neither of them spoke for a long time. He looked abstractedly at the passing houses and kept squeezing away at her fingers.

'What does your mother think about you being . . . well . . . you know . . . mixed up . . .?"

He looked shocked.

'God, I couldn't tell her a thing like that! She'd have a fit!' He grinned. 'I'll tell her when it's over. When we've won. I've a brother in the army. He fought through the war. He's a sergeant now. He tried to persuade me to join up when he was home on leave a couple of months ago. He said I'd like the life. He's a decent enough skin.'

'What did you say?'

'I said nothing on earth would persuade me to take the King's shilling and my mother said better the King's shilling than nobody's shilling at all. That's Declan. My sister's called Madge and she works in Clery's. I'm the youngest. The bad one.'

'Now I know.'

'Yes. Now you know.'

The tram stopped and the conductor rattled on his bell to tell everyone to get off.

'Dalkey,' he shouted. 'Dalkey.' He jumped down and began to transfer the trolley arm from one end of the tram to the other.

Nancy and Joe were the only passengers left on top. They went down the stairs. The driver was standing on his platform reading a newspaper.

'Do you know the way to the station?' Joe asked her, as they stepped down on to the road.

She nodded.

'I'll go back on this tram, so . . . if you're all right.'

'Of course I'm all right. It's been . . . I'm grand.'

He took hold of her arm just above the elbow. His fingers were able to stretch right round it. He pulled her very close to him.

'Will you be seeing him?'

She nodded.

'Well tell him . . . not today, don't go today . . .'

'Tell him?'

'That Broy says he must move on. He thinks it would be best.'

'Br . . .'

He squeezed her arm to prevent her from saying the name.

'Ow!'

'Just say that to him.'

He let go of her and took a step towards the tram. He turned back and looked at her. She was rubbing her arm.

'Did I hurt you?'

'Not really.'

'Nancy is a pretty name. I'll see you again, Nancy. Mind yourself.'

'And you.'

'I will. I'll turn up again, remember.'

'Like a bad penny.'

'Yeah. What's my name?'

'Joe Mulhare.'

'Say it again.'

'Joe Mulhare.'

'I'll see you, Nancy.'

He stepped up on to the platform. They stood looking at each other; she wished she had something to give him. She lifted her hand to her forehead in a salute.

'Au revoir.'

'Nancy,' was all he said, and ran up the winding stairs.

Harry was on the train. Aware of the possibility, she had been on the lookout for him as the train slowly moved into the station. Wispy fingers of steam grasped at the descending passengers' feet as the doors banged open. She saw him sitting in the corner of a first-class carriage, his head bent slightly towards a folded copy of the *Irish Times*. His city hat was sitting neatly on his knee. She climbed quickly into the third-class carriage next door, relieved that she hadn't been seen. When they arrived, she waited until he had got down from his carriage, his hat now firmly planted on his head, and had walked some way down the platform, before she got out herself. She watched him begin to climb the steep steps of the metal bridge that crossed the line. His long legs climbed quickly from step to step. Mrs Bradley from the hotel puffed behind him with a wicker basket over her arm. The engine driver let loose a great ball of steam that rose and hid the centre of the bridge. Harry disappeared into the cloud. Doors slammed. The porter walked along the platform securing the handles. The guard blew his whistle. The green flag waved; with a jerk and the usual rattling the train moved forward. Nancy ran up the steps and over the bridge. It trembled under her feet. The carriages slid away, running smoothly now. The smoke drifted back into the station and up into the evening sky. Harry was waiting for her at the door out into the road.

'Nancy.'

'Oh, hello there.'

She swung the bag with the library books in it with bravado.

'What on earth were you up to this afternoon?'

The sun was sideways and warm on their faces. A cool breeze blew from the sea. She watched the train gathering speed along the track curving towards the point. The sun glittered in the windows.

'I wasn't up to anything.'

'That chap you were with, who was he?'

Nancy didn't answer.

'He looks a terrible little tyke.'

Nancy swung the bag.

'Nancy?'

'Oh, I just met him in the library. He was changing books for his mother. We just happened to be going in the same direction. That sort of thing happens, you know.'

'He didn't look like someone whose mother would be getting books from the library. He didn't look as if his mother would be able to read. Where were you going on the tram?'

'I like trams,' she said truthfully.

'That's not an answer to my question.'

She did not say anything. The train had almost reached the point. Mushrooms of smoke drifted back towards them.

'It's really none of your business,' she said at last.

'I think perhaps I should have a word with Mary.'

'That's your business, I suppose. Interfering with my life. Why don't you do something with your own life instead of bothering with mine. Chuff chuff up to town in the morning, chuff chuff down in the evening, selling blooming stocks and shares or whatever it is you do in the middle. Where does all that get you?'

'It's a damn good job. One of the better jobs. You don't realise how lucky I was to get into the firm. I mean to say, after the war there were hundreds of chaps like me looking for work. I didn't even have the advantage of a couple of years at the university. I went slap into the army straight from school. If my father hadn't known Peter Jordan, I might be looking for a job yet.'

'I'm sure Mr Casey would find you something good in the property development line.'

'You are a little bitch, Nancy.'

'Oooooh!'

'I'm sorry. I didn't mean that.'

'Of course you did, and you're probably right.'

She bent down and took off her good shoes and dropped them in the bag with the books.

126

'I can't bear them another second. They're agony.'
. She pulled up her skirt and unfastened her stockings and
peeled them off. His face was very angry. His eyes watched
her movements to begin with and then shifted to the high
green hedge on their right. She rolled the stockings together
and put them in her pocket.
'That's better.'
'I want a decent life. That's all. A decent normal life. You
haven't the faintest idea what life is about.'
'Aspirations and things like that.'
'All you seem to want is trouble. And if there isn't any
trouble you'll make it. When you grow up, you'll see what
I mean. You'll realise. You'll settle down.'
She sighed.
. 'Anyway we've got off the point. Who was the little
tyke?'
'I've told you, he isn't a tyke . . .'
She turned and walked slowly away from him down the
road. The ground was warm still, and gritty under her feet.
'Why don't you take off that silly hat?'
He followed her, banging the *Irish Times* crossly against
his right leg as he walked.
'His mother is bedridden . . . temporarily . . . you understand. He had to fetch her . . .' She turned round to face
him, her ingenuous blue eyes gazing straight into his
face. She continued to walk, unfalteringly, backwards,
'. . . books. You can't after all languish in bed with nothing
to read. They live in Monkstown, just by the tower, over-
looking the sea. He left her lying looking out of the window.
Don't be too long, dear, she said, as he left the room. Come
straight home. We went on the tram together. I went on
to Dalkey and got the train from there. He paid my fare.
Wasn't that nice of him? Yes, he got her *Hamlet* . . .'
'*Hamlet?*'
'Oh, other things too. Emmm . . . *Great Expectations* . . .'
'All right. All right. You'll fall down if you go on walking
backwards like that.'
They had reached the gates. Nancy stopped.
'She'd just had her appendix out.'
'He didn't look the right sort. I hope . . .'

'Oh no, we didn't arrange to meet again or anything like that. We just said goodbye.' She giggled. 'I said thanks for paying my fare. Here we are.'

'Yes.'

She moved towards him.

'Is that all right, what I told you?'

'I suppose so.'

She smiled at him. She longed to touch his face with the tips of her fingers and feel his warm smooth flesh, but she didn't dare. She smiled even harder at him. At last he smiled back.

'You'll come up and have a drink? Aunt Mary'll be raging if you don't.'

'You are so exasperating.'

She took his arm and they walked up the avenue in silence.

Aunt Mary was leaning on the terrace wall waiting for them.

'You've been ages. I thought you must have missed the train.'

'We've been having a lovely row,' said Nancy.

'Poor Harry! He'll need a drink. Do take off that silly hat, Harry dear.'

Harry pulled his arm away from Nancy and took off his hat. He looked most put out.

'Apart from anything else,' said Aunt Mary, 'you'll be bald by the time you're forty. It's such a ridiculous habit men have.'

They climbed up the steps towards her.

'After all, God gave you a very good thatch. I hope, dear child, you didn't stroll around Dublin city in your bare feet.'

'I couldn't bear them another minute. I took them off down the road. I'll just go and change. I'll be down in a minute.'

She went into the house and ran upstairs.

'Mary,' the old man's voice was calling. 'Mary, Mary, Mary.'

She closed her bedroom door carefully. Drifting up from the terrace she could hear Aunt Mary's voice rushing along as if too much had to be said in too short a time. Harry laughed. That was good anyway. She took her notebook

128

from the drawer and opened it at a clean page. Joe Mulhare, she wrote. Full stop. Joe Mulhare. joe mulhare. JOE MULHARE. Joe. joe, joe. Joe Mulhare.

Nancy spent the morning picking fruit and vegetables for Bridie. The last of the loganberries, which grew against the high grey wall of the garden and had to be stretched for. Tiny prickles scraped at her arms and juice from the berries stained her fingers purple. Then she sat on a stool in the yard outside the kitchen and podded peas into a white china bowl. Swallows preened above her on the wires and swooped and darted from time to time through the broken windows of the yard buildings. The cat was stretched in the middle of the yard, his expectant eyes watchful. She hoped he wouldn't mind the move. Cats were funny creatures; perhaps he would keep coming back and back here, finding his way across the hills from Laragh, or perhaps he might pine away and die, lonely for his own haunts, his swallows, his mice, his enemies, with whom he fought at night. Bridie would be very upset if anything were to happen to him. She would miss his company in the kitchen, the long conversations of miaows and words that they each seemed to enjoy. Would it be possible that Aunt Mary too might pine away, her roots like the cat's too old for transplanting? My most beautiful and tender memories will always be of this place, even this simple moment – the drone of bees, the smell through the kitchen door of baking bread, the shadows on the cobblestones, Bridie rattling her sweeping brush out of an upstairs window. I have inside me that gentleness, that calm, from which to begin to explore the real life that waits. I can never be undermined because of that. Maybe that is just hopefulness. Though nothing will ever be the same, I can draw on the strength that this way of living has given me, like Joe Mulhare can draw his strength from the image of his father.

'Have you got them peas done yet?'

Bridie bustled and creaked out through the door. The cat whisked his tail in some sort of salutation.

'Nearly.'

'Well get a move on with them. She wants her lunch on

129

time. It's her golf afternoon.'

She bent down and picked up a handful of pods from the basket and ran her thumbnail along the spine of one of them, tumbling the peas into the bowl. 'They're good the peas this year. Last year they were bullets. I never understand.'

Nancy put a pea in her mouth and bit the sweet juice out of it.

'Will you mind leaving here, Bridie?'

Plink, plink, plink, plink. The peas dropped swiftly from her short flat fingers. 'It's all the one to me where I am. Why should I mind?'

'You might miss your friends and things like that.'

'I might if it was America I was skiting off to, or over the water even. But it's only down the road. I'm fully occupied wherever I am. It's young ones like you that sits around with their heads in the clouds taking half an hour to shell a few peas that has to fret about things like that.'

'I'm not fretting.'

Plink, plink, plink.

'I'm glad of that. You've all your life in front of you and God is good.'

Plink.

'Did you know my father, Bridie?'

There was a short pause.

'I did.'

Plink, plink, plink.

'And then again I didn't.'

The cat sat up and began to scratch its ear.

'Full of charm. Airy fairy. If that's what you were going to ask me?'

'Something like that.'

Plink, plink.

'There you have it.'

'It's not much to go on really.'

'Here one minute, gone the next. That was the make of him. Unreliable, I'd have said, if anyone had asked me.'

'Miaow!'

'He wants his dinner. He came from abroad . . .'

'He was foreign?' Nancy was startled.

'Not at all. He came from the West somewhere, Clare, I think, but he came here from abroad. He had a lot of funny ideas and he went off abroad again. After the wedding. He never came back after that at all. I think She said he was killed somewhere. I don't know . . .' She frowned as she thought back. 'India. Would that be right? India, I think it was.'

Plink, plink, plink.

'India.'

'How amazing!' She thought of him stretched in the moonlight beside the Taj Mahal.

'He was a travelling sort of man. Not one for marrying at all.'

'Why did he then, I wonder?'

Bridie sighed. 'He had to see her right. He was a gentleman, if nothing else. Maybe if she hadn't died he'd have come back some time, if God had spared him. Maybe he would and maybe he wouldn't.'

Nancy digested this. The cat stood up on its toes and danced around a little.

'Do you mean I'm . . .' She paused, wondering how to put it so she wouldn't upset Bridie.

'I always told her you'd ask one day, and there's no point in telling lies, and what of it anyway?'

The bowl was full. Bridie stooped and gathered up the pods from the ground into her large white apron.

'I suppose,' said Nancy at last, 'they loved each other.'

'I suppose they did. What would they want to do that for if they didn't? Bring the bowl into the kitchen while I get on with the lunch. You seem to think I've nothing to do but gab.'

One of her hands held the apron bunched in front of her; with the other one she touched Nancy on the shoulder.

'What of it anyway?' she repeated. 'You're young and you've been well rared. We all love you.'

Nancy nodded. Bridie's hand was heavy on her shoulder. A whole weight of years of love and people giving and taking.

'God is good.' The words sighed out of Bridie's mouth as if for once she might have had doubts. She moved into the

131

darkness of the house.

'Don't go bothering Her,' she called back, her voice confident once more, 'about that sort of thing. She's enough bothers on her as it is and bring in them peas.'

He was lying on the beach when she arrived at the hut. Quite motionless, like a cat. His eyes stared up at the floating clouds. He had taken off his shirt and neatly tucked it under the back of his neck, and she could see that a long puckered scar disfigured his thin body. It ran from just below his collarbone down the left-hand side of his chest and disappeared inside his trousers.

'Hail fellow well met, All dirty and wet; Find out if you can, who's master, who's man.'

He didn't move, just spoke the words up towards the clouds.

'How did you know it was me?'

'I', he corrected gently. 'Disrespect for the language does no service to the world.'

'Who said that anyway?'

She sat down beside him.

'Said what?'

'That . . . hail fellow . . . I've always heard it.'

'The mad Dean. The chap who invented your name. I knew it was you, dear child, because no matter how hard you try to creep up on me, you haven't yet got control of your arms and legs . . . in fact I may as well say here and now that I hope you never have to make your living by creeping up on people.'

He stared at the clouds and she stared at the sea, which changed in colour from green to blue to grey with each movement of the waves.

'How did you get that scar?'

'These wounds I had on Crispin's day.'

Silence.

She turned and looked at him. He had a faint smile on his face.

'Ypres. Wipers. The young man, boy I should say, he was about your age, I was with was hit by a shell. I've never worked out which of us was the lucky one.'

132

'It's horrible!'

He put out his hand and took hers. He ran her fingers all the way down the scar, pressing them into the soft puckered flesh. Her fingers cringed away from the feel of it, but he held them tight and wouldn't let them go. Down under the top of his trousers to the hard jutting bone of his hip and then back again up to his shoulder. Then down again. His ribs moved gently like a calm, rippling sea. The scar itself was quite unlike the grainy flesh around it to touch; it was like a long, macabre mouth, with the pale marks of stitching criss-crossing the lips, pulling it awkwardly together. He let go of her hand.

'Horrible!' she said again.

She looked down at her fingers, which had never touched anything like that before.

'Now,' he ordered, 'you do it. You touch it yourself.'

Gently she ran her fingers up to his shoulder.

'You see.'

She buried her fingers in the sand. The top layer was warm and dry, but below the surface it was cold and damp and abrasive.

'I take it your journey yesterday went according to plan.'

She nodded.

'Joe . . .'

'I make a point of never knowing people's names.'

'I liked him. We went on a tram.'

'A tram is a very fine invention.'

'He said to tell you that . . . Broy says that he thinks you ought to move on. It would be best.'

'Ah!'

He sat up and dusted the sand from his shoulders. She wondered if he were going to move on then and there.

'If you go into the hut,' he said, 'and feel in the pocket of my coat, you'll find the whisky. I think we should have a drink.'

When she came out with the bottle and two mugs, he was sitting there with his shirt on once more, neatly buttoned up as far as the collar stud.

'Is that more acceptable? Not very, I fear. My father always said that no gentleman should appear in public with

133

his neck unclothed.'

'I'm hardly public.'

She handed him the bottle. She knelt beside him, holding the two mugs out towards him. He opened the bottle and poured carefully.

'I suppose this means you'll go away?'

He nodded.

'In a day or two.'

'Where will you go?'

'Away.'

'I wish that occasionally you'd answer one of my questions.'

'You always ask the wrong ones.'

'Will you come back?'

He took a drink from his mug.

'Not here.'

'So I will never see you again?'

'Probably not.'

'I don't like that.'

'You'll get over it.'

'I wish you didn't have to kill people.'

'Somebody has to.'

'I really don't understand why.'

'You will one day.'

'And there is no hope without it?'

'No.'

She made a hollow in the sand for her mug.

'May a daughter kiss her father goodbye?'

She crept right up beside him. He put his arms around her and held her close to him. One heart seemed to beat in both their bodies. His cheek against hers was abrasive as the sand had been.

'You won't let them catch you, will you?'

'I intend to die in my bed, child, with my bottle of claret.'

He let go of her and looked carefully at her face.

'I must be getting old.'

'Why do you say that?'

'Because for the first time in many years I regret having to say goodbye.'

The radiance of the smile she gave him made him tremble.

'What a lovely thing to say to me!'

'It won't be the last time that men say that sort of thing to you. I mean it. Now drink your drink, child, and go.'

'I don't want it, thank you.'

'I'll leave everything as I found it.'

'Don't worry . . .'

'I'd rather you didn't come down here for three or four days. Make it a week.'

'A week,' she repeated.

He held his hand out to her. She shook it very formally.

'Goodbye.'

'Goodbye, Nancy. Oh, by the way . . .'

'Yes?'

'Joe Mulhare is a good young man. Remember that if you meet him again.'

'Yes.'

She climbed up through the blocks, and when she got to the line, she turned and looked back. He was sitting as he had sat before, staring out to sea. He didn't move.

Friday Evening

I think I'll stop writing in this book. I find it harder and harder to put down in words my direct thoughts about what happens day by day. It seems to me that I will have to work out some sort of filtering system in order to put ideas clearly on to paper. You have to work these things out for yourself. Everything perhaps. Yes. Now that I know that my father is dead, I will have more room and time. I will never know now whether his second toe is slightly longer than his first one. I don't mind about his death nor do I mind about my own anomalous situation. As Bridie said . . . what of it? I thought I would mind forever. Maybe when I am old and sitting by the fire, I will pick it up all over again and worry and wonder. Now there is no time. It is hard to be young and not quite grasp what it is you are trying to understand, but exciting. I have felt lifted by some excitement or other in the last few days. Like being on the edge of an earthquake.

I have to look after Grandfather tomorrow while Aunt Mary and the two Miss Brabazons go racing. I hope he won't be too potty.

The Daimler drove away down the avenue about midday, filled with the three ladies in hats and gloves, a picnic hamper and a bottle of gin. The wind was soft and rain promising, though the sun was shining brightly. Round the horizon great piles of clouds waited their moment.

Nancy and the old man ate their lunch in silence, and then she pushed him to the window and placed the glasses on his knee. He smiled courteously .'Thank you, my dear.'

She took a cushion and went out on to the terrace and sat down with her back against the warm grey wall of the house. She could hear the intermittent crooning of his voice and the wheezing that came from his lungs when he moved. Down at the bottom of the hill Maeve was at the piano again. Nancy wondered if Harry were there, sitting on the floral sofa, wearing his adoring, listening face.

'*Probablement*,' she whispered, and smiled at the idiotic sound of the word. She must have fallen asleep, because when Grandfather called to her, she gave a little jump of surprise.

'Child.'

'Oh!'

'We didn't wear khaki when I was a young man.'

The clouds were moving now across the sky, still high, obscuring the sun from time to time.

'No. No.'

He raised his glasses once more and lapsed into silence.

She frowned down towards the railway. Nothing moved.

'That was of course when I was a young man. Later on things changed. Everything changed.'

A large raindrop burst on the ground beside her.

'Things change.'

She got up and brought the cushion into the house.

'Change and decay in all around I see,' he sang.

She closed the window down.

'Khaki.'

She laid the dining-room table for Bridie. The white lace mats neatly framed by the silver forks and spoons and knives always gave her pleasure. A large bowl of roses filled the room with scent. The rain began to pour down, blowing in through the open windows and scattering drops on the floor. Bridie ran out into the yard to bring in the washing, piling the white towels and tablecloths over her shoulder as she pulled them off the line. 'Glory be, glory be!' she panted. The cat sat in a doorway scornfully, lazily watching her panic. Nancy went back into the drawing-room.

'Will I bring you over to the fire, Grandfather? You won't be able to see anything till that goes over.'

137

'No, no,' he said, irritated at the thought of having to be moved. 'The rain will pass. I will be able to watch again. Steam rises up from the earth after the rain has passed.'

'Not here, Grandfather, only in hot countries.'

'Yes. Hot countries. Did I ever tell you that we were the first up Talana Hill?'

She shook her head and wondered where Talana Hill had been.

'It was a hard fight. We lost a lot of men and then, from behind, our own artillery began firing on us.'

'Oh Grandfather, how terrible!'

'Yes. Terrible. Terrible would be the only word. Hold your fire. I stood up right up in the middle of it when I realized what was happening. Hold your fire. I held my arms up in the air in the hopes . . . hold your fire. It wasn't any use. The Boers were bad enough, but that . . . we lost . . . I don't remember.'

'Was that where you got your field glasses?'

'I beg your . . .?'

'Your glasses. You told me you got them from a man in a shell hole.'

'Ridiculous.' He thought for a while. 'I can't . . . the picture has gone. It was . . .' His head fell forward for a moment, and then with an effort he pulled it up again.

'It is very demoralizing to be fired upon by your own men.'

'It would be.'

'I can't remember. Where is Mary?'

'She's at the Curragh. She'll be back for dinner.'

'I should have died there.'

'Oh Grandfather, don't say such silly things.'

'Brave days!'

His head drooped again and this time his eyes also drooped, and soon he was asleep.

The rain stayed. Thick and low the clouds swooped. Soon I'll be able to touch them, she thought, feel their softness, squeeze them in my fist and watch the water seeping out through my fingers.

Seven o'clock came and went and there was no sign of the Daimler.

The old man allowed himself to be pushed over to the

138

fire, where he sat and sang to himself, beating time with his frail hand. Nancy sat in the corner of the sofa reading. Bridie fussed in and out of the hall and along the passage to the kitchen.

'They should have gone in Her car. She's never late back.'

'There's probably been a hold-up of some sort. They'll be here at any minute.'

'It's not like Her.'

'No.'

'If they're not here soon, the dinner'll be ruined on them, so it will be.'

'You're fussing, Bridie.'

'I am not fussing. Only who gets the blame if the dinner's ruined?'

'Fuss, fuss.'

'I hope they haven't had an accident.'

'It's a long drive from the Curragh.'

'Them motors.'

She marched down the passage again, her shoes squeaking with each angry step. Nancy wandered to the hall door and looked out at the grey avenue, grey trees, grey grass.

'Chiaroscuro. That's what it is.'

She thought of Talana Hill, wherever it was, and the men in khaki shooting each other, and the heaps of khaki dead on the grey stony hillside. She wondered if it had been a hill like the hill at the back of the house. Inhospitable, she supposed, with grey slippery rocks and steaming earth. Unlike here, where the whitethorn and fuchsia hedges would hide the frightened men from other frightened men, and the beech wood would shelter them from the sun. But then of course the shells would rip through the hedges and uproot the beech trees, and then the two hills might look the same.

'Is there any sign?' Bridie interrupted her nightmare.

'Sister Anne, Sister Anne, is there anyone coming?'

'What's that?'

'No sign.' But as she spoke, the Daimler came round the bend in the avenue and the horn growled.

'Here they are.'

'God is good.' The car drew up outside the door and the three ladies climbed out.

'Hurray!' said Nancy. 'You're terribly late. Bridie's going a little potty.'

She looked at their faces. 'What's the matter? What's happened?'

Aunt Mary was pale and old. Red lines ringed her eyes as if she had been crying. The small Miss Brabazon, as usual, put out her hand to be shaken. 'We've had the most terrible time!'

'An accident . . . ?'

'Oh God, no!' said Miss Celia. 'We'll tell you all when we've cleaned ourselves up a bit and had a drink. Mary's a bit shaken. Aren't you, dear?'

'Yes. We're all a bit shaken, I think. It's all right, Nancy. Nothing to worry about. We . . . we're all right.'

'I refuse to hang about. My bladder won't hold out much longer.' Miss Celia dashed up the stairs, followed more sedately by the other two.

They came down eventually looking more composed. The old man opened his eyes as they came into the room. 'Ah, Mary!' He paid no heed to the visitors. 'My rug has slipped.'

Aunt Mary kissed his cheek and bent to rearrange his rug.

'Celia, dear, get everyone a drink, will you? There pet, that should keep the draughts out. Have you had a good day?'

'There were soldiers in the field.'

'Goodness gracious!'

She patted him soothingly on the arm.

'I saw them.'

'That must have been interesting. Something new for you to look at.'

'We didn't wear khaki when . . .'

'Do tell me what happened . . . I'm dying of curiosity.'

'Good, strong drinks,' said Miss Celia, handing them round. 'Nancy?'

'I'll get myself a glass of sherry, thank you. Don't you bother.'

Aunt Mary and Miss George settled themselves by the fire. Miss Celia paced the room, sometimes holding her glass at such an angle that the whisky slopped out on to the carpet.

'The most awful thing happened . . .' began Aunt Mary.

'Let me tell her.'

'Oh Celia, you weren't there. Not with us.'

'We'll all have to tell you little bits. You start, Mary.'

'It was just after the third race . . .'

'Starting to spot with rain.'

'But looking awfully black.'

'And I thought,' said Aunt Mary, as if neither of the others had spoken, 'that I'd better go and get my macintosh from the motor.'

'And so did I, and Celia, who never minds getting wet, stayed behind talking to Freddy Hennessy . . .'

'Just looked like a shower to me.'

'We took a few minutes to get to the motor . . .'

'We always try to park near the road, it's so much easier to get out. We'd just got there . . .'

'This man . . . a soldier and a young girl passed us . . .'

'His wife.'

'That doesn't matter.'

'Yes, it matters. A pretty girl. Young. They were hurrying, they didn't want to get wet. Laughing . . .'

'Oh George, do let Mary get on!'

'Details are important.'

'What happened?' asked Nancy.

Grandfather appeared to be listening. His eyes moved from one speaker to the other. 'A soldier,' he said.

'Well, we got to the motor and I was standing there while George was opening the door. A man came out from behind the motor . . .'

'From behind our car. Our Daimler. He must have been waiting there.'

'I saw him casually walking. He had something in his hand . . . I didn't see. I wasn't really looking . . . I wouldn't have expected . . .'

'I was searching for my brolly.'

'And then there was this bang and the soldier was lying on the ground. Just like that. I didn't really know what had happened. There was this bang.'

'I said "What's that bang, Mary?" and she didn't answer and then the girl suddenly started to scream.'

'It was all most peculiar, as if the world had stopped for a moment. I can't explain. We went over to them. Ran really once we realized that something awful had happened. There was no sign of the man. Only the girl screaming and the . . .'

'Dead.'

'Dead? Oh how dreadful!'

'There wasn't any blood. You always expect blood.'

'Well, there was a little.'

'I put my macintosh over him in case he was cold.'

'My dear Mary, he wouldn't have needed that if he were dead,' said Celia.

'I had to do something. I thought he might be cold and wet and well . . . then suddenly there were hundreds of people all around us and the poor girl . . .'

'Screaming her head off. "Slap her," I said to Mary. It's the only thing to do. But Mary just stood there as if she were planted and I couldn't bring myself to slap her.'

'Hundreds of people . . . and then we heard the other shots and then a sort of panic took over.'

'Not where we were. We were just at the paddock gate and we heard these poppings. "Funny," Freddy said, "just like shots," and I said don't be a blithering idiot, not that he can help it. Anyway no one paid any attention. Then a few minutes later someone said that General Macready had been murdered and then someone else said they'd caught and killed Michael Collins. All sorts of idiotic things people were saying and I thought I'd better go and look for the others. Freddy insisted on coming too and we found them, and crowds, and police and soldiers, and the poor young man lying there covered with Mary's macintosh.'

'What happened to the wife?'

'We tried to get her to sit in the Daimler, out of the rain at least, but she wouldn't. She sat on the grass beside him until some woman came along and took her away.'

'And him,' said Aunt Mary. 'They took him away too.'

'And Mary's macintosh.'

'I wouldn't have wanted it again anyway.'

'And the other shots? . . . Were they . . . ?'

'Twelve soldiers dead. They must have been following each one of them. No one was caught.'

'Then the police kept us for ages asking questions.'

'I really didn't see what the man looked like. He just had a hat and a coat on like everyone else. That's all I could tell them.'

'I didn't see him at all.'

'She was looking for her brolly.'

'But they kept asking the same questions over and over again. And it rained.'

'You should have had a bath, Mary, when you got back.'

'I was perfectly dry by then.'

'The chaos was terrible, with everyone trying to get home.'

'I didn't see what he had in his hand.'

'Even if you had, dear, what could you have done?'

'Dinner is ready,' announced Bridie. 'And it won't wait.'

'Thank you, Bridie. We'll be straight in. We've had a terrible day.'

'I heard. Jimmy heard in the village and he came out to tell me. That's twelve less English soldiers to torture our poor boys.'

'That's a point of view, Bridie. Just one point of view.'

'It's my point of view.'

'And it's my point of view,' said Nancy to her own surprise.

'My dear Nancy, you know nothing about it at all.'

'I'm learning.'

'Don't be cheeky to your aunt, she's had a hard day. If the dinner's spoiled, yez have only yourselves to blame.' She turned and made her creaking way back to the kitchen.

No one wanted to talk during dinner. No one really seemed to want to eat either, but fear of bringing Bridie's anger round their heads made them all do their best. The old man beat out the tune of whatever song he was singing in his head with a finger on the edge of the table. The three women's faces were stiff with loneliness and unease. From time to time Miss George coughed politely into her small lace handkerchief.

'I suppose,' said Aunt Mary, 'you shouldn't say things like that, Nancy.'

'Like what?'

'That ... about your point of view. You are too young to understand these things.'

'I don't think you understand them very well either, so you shouldn't really criticize me.'

She blushed after she had spoken.

Miss Celia Brabazon put her spoon and fork neatly together on her plate.

'Ireland unfree will never be at peace,' she quoted.

'Gabriel wore that uniform. I thought of him when I saw that poor young man lying there.'

'Gabriel died fighting someone else's war.'

'But this isn't a war.'

'Of course it's a war, Mary dear, whether you like it or not, and one day you're going to have to decide which side you're on. Nancy, for what it's worth, seems to have made her decision.'

The small Miss Brabazon stood up.

'I think we should go home, Celia. We're all tired and upset. We should go to bed. I want to go to bed. I don't want to talk about war and death and decisions, and I'm sure Mary doesn't either.'

The doorbell rang.

The room was dark and in the candlelight their faces hung like golden carvings around the table. They listened in silence to Bridie's footsteps as they marched along the passage and across the hall. She opened the door and they could hear the low murmur of voices. Her steps came towards them, and, as she opened the dining-room door, the room was invaded by the light from the hall. The candles flickered.

'Mam.'

'Yes Bridie, who is it?'

'Them.'

Bridie's voice was sepulchral. Nancy felt like bursting out laughing.

'Do put on the light till we see where we are.'

Bridie touched the switch and they all blinked. Standing

in the doorway was an officer, cap in hand.

'Miss Dwyer?' He looked around the table.

'We're just finishing dinner,' said Aunt Mary, somewhat unnecessarily.

'I'm sorry to disturb you.'

'Do come in. What can I do for you?'

'My fellows are outside having a look round. I just wondered if I could have a word with you. Captain Rankin is my name.'

'Good evening, Captain. Miss Celia Brabazon, Miss Georgina Brabazon, my father General Dwyer and my niece Nancy.'

He bowed.

The old man had stopped drumming on the table and was looking the soldier up and down.

'Mary . . .'

'Yes, darling?'

'What's that fellow doing here?'

'He's just come to ask a few questions.' She turned to the young man. 'My father's not quite himself. You'll have to excuse him.'

'I told you I saw soldiers all over the place today.'

'I expect you've heard about today's tragedy, Miss Dwyer?'

The tall Miss Brabazon stood up and walked across the room towards him. She held out her hand.

'We must offer our sympathies. Please accept . . .'

He took her hand and held it for a moment.

'Thank you.'

'Now, if we may, we must go. George. We've had a terrible, bloody day.'

George moved towards the door. As she passed Aunt Mary, she put her hand on her shoulder.

'Go to bed early. Don't let anyone stop you from doing that. We will ring you on the telephone tomorrow. You see,' she explained to the soldier, 'we were there. We saw . . .'

'I'll come to the door,' said Aunt Mary, getting up. 'Please excuse me for a moment.'

The three women left the room. Nancy stared out of the

window. How silly the poor flickering candles looked now that the light was on! She watched their movement in the window. The soldier stood quite still just inside the door, cap in hand.

'Gabriel. What happened to Gabriel?'

Nancy wondered if he wanted a reply. The voices of the women drifted into the room.

'Talana Hill. Maybe he went at Talana Hill.'

'No,' said Nancy. 'Not Gabriel.'

The hall door banged. 'Were you by any chance at Talana Hill? You. You, young man.'

'No, sir. I . . .'

Aunt Mary came into the room.

'I'm sorry. There are soldiers in the yard, Bridie says.'

'They're my men. We're just having a look round. You see, we're looking for this man . . .'

'I hope they won't upset Bridie.'

'I don't think . . . It's a routine search. It's for your safety, too. You see, he could be armed. Dangerous.'

Nancy stood up.

'I think I'll go to bed.'

'I'd rather you stayed. I've a few questions to ask. Only a minute or two.'

'Yes, dear. You must stay. You're looking for a man, you say?'

He took a photograph out of his pocket and handed it to her.

'This is the man. Have you by any chance seen him around here? We believe him to be in this neighbourhood. We have been looking for him for a very long time.'

There was a long silence while Aunt Mary studied the picture in her hand. Nancy pushed her hands into the pockets of her cardigan and hoped they wouldn't still be shaking when the photograph was passed to her.

Aunt Mary shook her head slowly. 'It's strange. The face rings a bell. Oh, very far away. No I haven't seen that man. No.'

'Are you sure? It's very important.'

'I'm sure. It could be a face from the very distant past. Or not. I'm not sure.'

146

'Could you name the man?'

Aunt Mary handed him back the picture.

'No . . . I couldn't do that.'

'General . . .' He approached the old man with the picture in his hand.

'He never goes out. Never beyond the terrace. There would be no point in asking him anything. He spends most of the time asleep.'

Grandfather's head had fallen forward on to his chest. His eyes, though half open, saw nothing.

'Miss . . . er . . . Nancy?'

Nancy didn't take her hands out of her pockets. She looked down without moving at the photograph that the soldier had put on the table beside her. It was Cassius. Dressed in the uniform of a major, he stood by the door of an old stone cottage. The sun was shining and his eyes were slightly screwed up against the glare. In one hand he held a short cane. He looked very fit, as if he intended to live a long time.

'No.' Her voice had no tremor.

'He wouldn't of course be dressed like that. Not now.'

She shook her head.

'No.'

'Are you sure?'

'I'm sure.'

Carefully he put the picture back into his top pocket.

'If by any chance you do see him, or a stranger, round the place, would you let us know, or the police. It is very important.'

'He is a very dangerous man,' said Aunt Mary in a matter of fact way.

'He is an organiser. An invisible man. A vicious, ruthless rebel.'

'Goodness gracious!'

His face reddened.

'It would be in your own interest to assist. In every way. We strongly suspect he planned this atrocity this afternoon.'

'We will do what we can, Captain Rankin. I'm sorry we haven't been of more help to you.'

147

'I won't disturb you any longer. Good night.'

'I saw a man on the railway line.'

As Grandfather spoke, Nancy turned and looked once more at the reflections in the window. She watched the soldier turn and move back to the old man.

'Sir?'

'A man on the railway line.'

'Oh Father dear, you do carry on so!'

'When would this have been, sir?'

She watched him fumble in his pocket for the photograph. The old man shook his head.

'I don't remember.'

'In the last few days? Today perhaps? Here, could this be the man?'

He pushed the picture into the old man's hand. He stared at it for a long time. 'That's not my son,' he said. 'That's not Gabriel.'

'Darling, of course it's not Gabriel.'

She crossed the room and took the picture from his fingers. She handed it back to the soldier.

'I told you, he sees nothing except what he imagines. You'll upset him. You mustn't do that. Please go now.'

'Ask Nancy,' said the old man. 'She was talking to him.'

Nancy turned back towards them.

'That was only an old tramp. I told you that. It was old Forty Coats.'

'When would this have been, Miss Nancy?'

'I don't really remember. A couple of days ago. It was Forty Coats. He's always hanging around.'

'On the railway line?'

'Well, yes. Anywhere. He comes and goes. He's a tramp.'

'He's been wandering round since I was a child,' said Aunt Mary. 'He's quite harmless.'

'That's who Grandfather saw me talking to.'

'Would that be correct, sir?'

'Correct?'

'Would it be this tramp Forty Coats that you saw talking to Miss Nancy on the line?'

'Mary?'

'I think it must have been, pet.'

'Very well.'

He waved his hand in a dismissive way at the soldier, as he might have done twenty years before.

'Very well then.'

The young man bowed to Aunt Mary and then to Nancy.

'Nancy, will you see Captain Rankin to the door? I must put Father to bed.'

They crossed the hall without saying a word. She opened the door. He stepped out and put his cap on. Away beyond the railway the moonlight made a bright path on the sea.

'Good night,' he said.

'Good night.'

When she went back into the dining room, Aunt Mary and Grandfather had gone. She switched off the light and pressed her hot forehead against the window. Eight or ten men in file moved down the avenue. It looked to her as if they were carrying rifles. Her head ached with fear. I suppose I've helped to kill twelve men, she thought. God forgive me for that. She thought of Aunt Mary covering the young man with her raincoat and then of Grandfather on Talana Hill being shot at by his own side. Hold your fire. If I could see the pattern, then maybe I could understand. There has to be a pattern. It can't all just be futile in the end.

'Mooning?' asked Aunt Mary, coming into the room behind her.

'I suppose so.'

'I'm going to have a very strong drink and then go to bed. Would you like one too?'

'No thanks.'

Aunt Mary came over and stood beside her. The moon silvered their faces. The soldiers were gone.

'I think it's a good thing we're leaving here. I wouldn't want you to be weighed down by my ghosts.'

There was a long silence. Two bats swooped and soared, like the swallows in the sunlight.

'It wasn't a tramp, was it?'

'No.'

She was glad she had said it.

'Old Forty Coats hasn't been around this way for a long time. I hope you're not doing anything you'll regret.'

'How do you ever know?'

Aunt Mary sighed. 'You don't.'

'The man in the picture? Who was he?'

'Perhaps I'm not right about him. His face is just one of the shadows in my mind. They used to live over near the Cherry Orchard. Barry was their name . . . The house was pulled down some time ago. Ages ago . . . Barry. They sort of died out. Angus was his name. We used to call him Angoose.' She smiled. 'They died out. Except for him. Mind you, I thought he was probably dead too. Killed like . . . well, so many. I'm glad to think he's still alive, even if . . .' A third bat joined its companions. If I were out there, Nancy thought, I would be able to hear them calling, but Aunt Mary wouldn't. 'I suppose I'll have to go up to town one day and find a suitable landlady for you. Someone who'll keep an eye on you and not let you go wandering round Dublin getting yourself into trouble. If such a person exists.'

'I suppose so.'

'We used to go to such lovely parties and balls and everyone seemed happy.'

'I don't suppose they were.'

'Bed.'

'Yes.'

'You don't want to tell me anything?'

'No.'

'Good night then.'

She went to get her strong drink.

She didn't turn on the light in her room, in case the bats came in through the open window. She sat on the side of her bed fully dressed waiting for the household sounds to fade away. It took a long time. Aunt Mary wandered restlessly from room to room, switching lights on and off, no doubt refilling her glass from time to time. Water rattled in the pipes, stair treads creaked, doors here and there opened quietly and closed again. Finally there was the quiet, breathing silence of night time. Bars of moonlight lay on the stairs as she went down. Outside there was only silver and deep black shadows; even the bats had gone. There seemed to be an emptiness. She ran across the fields and over the line and then down on to the sand. If they were watching the line, she thought . . . oh God, if they were watching the line! If they were watching . . . if . . . She ran straight down to the sea and then along through the edge of the freezing, rippling water, her feet stirring the phosphorescence as she ran.

There was no sign of life at the hut. The guardian seagull crouched down into its feathers on the roof. As she approached the door, she prayed that he would be gone, but he was there, lying in the corner, wrapped in the rug. She left the door open behind her and the silver light followed her into the darkness.

'I thought I told you not to come back.'

He sat up slowly and looked at her.

'I hoped you'd be gone. I think they'll be here in the morning. They've been everywhere asking questions, searching. Grandfather told them he saw a man on the line. He didn't mean any . . .'

'That's all right, Nancy. It was only a matter of time. I was going to go when it got light, now I'll go a bit earlier.'

He got up. He then bent down and picked up the rug; he shook it and folded it neatly. A small canvas army bag leaned against the wall.

'Where will you go?'

'Away.'

'Yes. I shouldn't have asked, should I?'

'I am a very secret person.'

'The soldier said you were dangerous.'

He laughed.

'Good. I like to be thought dangerous.'

'Those twelve . . .'

He moved towards her.

'I'm sorry, Nancy. They were dangerous too. Twelve new dangerous men. They had to be stopped before they did a lot of damage. We are very naïve people. These men were capable of finding out things that would have harmed a lot of people. Created problems. We have to win, Nancy. In the end of all, the people have to win. This is very important.'

151

'You make it sound important.'

Suddenly above them the bird on the roof awoke, It adjusted its position and flapped its wings for a few seconds. The it slowly took off and beat its way out to sea.

'I think you should go.'

'Yes.' He picked up the canvas bag.

'Are you Angus Barry?'

'What a very persistent young lady you are! I might have been. I certainly am no longer.'

'But could I think of you as that person?'

'If it gives you pleasure.'

He picked up her right hand and kissed it.

'So, with an Angus Barry gesture I leave you. I shall go along the coast a bit and then cut up into the hills. I will be all right. I have a place to go where I will be safe.'

She nodded.

'Will you stay here a little while after I have gone?'

'I'll make sure there are no signs left.' She smiled at him. 'I'll cover up for you.'

They moved to the door and stood close together looking out at the world.

'It's cold,' she said.

'It's always cold at this time of night.'

Somewhere up above the beach a stone tumbled. She clutched at his arm.

'Go.'

'Yes. I hope I haven't done you too much harm.'

'Just go.'

She stamped her foot.

He stepped out of the hut and began to walk towards the sea.

Her heart beat so hard she thought she would die there and then.

'Halt.'

A line of men materialized from the darkness, stretching from the railway right down to the edge of the sea. He walked on. His feet now splashed through the little white curling waves.

'Halt.'

The crunch of their feet on the sand. If he swam, he might

152

get away. She ran down the sand towards him.

'Run. They're here. Run. Swim. Please.'

'There's no point in running or swimming, Major Barry.'

He stopped walking and turned. The water was covering his good leather shoes.

'Go back, Nancy,' he said. 'Go back now. This minute.'

'They're here,' was all she could reply.

'Major Barry, we know you are armed. Throw your bag and your gun on to the sand. Don't do anything foolish. We won't hesitate to shoot both you and the girl if you do anything stupid.'

The man stood quite still.

'The girl knows nothing about this. She is a child. She brought me a few scraps of food from time to time. She knows nothing. Let her out of here. Safely out. Then, I swear, you can take me.'

'Oh no!'

'Gun and bag on the sand.'

'When you let the girl out. I'm not telling you a lie. The girl is irrelevant.'

'All right. The girl can go.'

She looked at him across the few feet between them. He smiled at her. 'Go now, Nancy. Just walk through them and keep on walking until you get home.'

'What will happen?'

'Nothing will happen. They will take me to prison. That's all. Turn round and walk.'

'Are you telling me the truth?'

'Yes.'

She nodded. She turned round and faced the soldiers. Their silver faces were indifferent.

'Goodbye.'

'Au revoir.'

'Thank you,' she said and started to walk.

She walked through the soldiers and up towards the blocks of stone, then she stopped and looked back. He had thrown his bag on to the sand and was fumbling in his pocket for the gun. He took it out and looked at it for a moment, and then threw it down beside the bag. Then they shot him. Two. Three shots. Running.

'No, no, no!'

Four. Five. Six. Making sure.

'Hold your fire.' She heard her voice screaming like Grandfather's at Talana Hill.

Running.

Seven.

Silence.

'No, no!'

They caught her just before she reached the body, stroked now by the gentle sea.

'No!'

Two men were leaning over him. Red in the waves, turning to pink, washing, cleaning the wounds.

'Keep him below the tide line. We don't want to have to clear up a mess.'

'Sir.'

'The boat'll be along in a minute.'

'Please,' she said to one of the men holding her. 'Please let me help him.'

He laughed. 'That poor sod don't need help no more.'

'Why? He said you'd put him in prison. Why?'

'Don't arsk me, lidy. We only obey orders.'

'Take that girl home, one of you. Back where she came from.'

'I can go home alone. I don't need anyone to take me.'

'Corporal Tweedie, take the girl home and tell her parents from us they ought to keep an eye on her.'

'Sir.'

The engine of a boat puttered in the distance.

'No,' she said.

'Come along with me, Miss.' Corporal Tweedie's voice was kind.

'What are you going to do with him?'

'You can let go of her now. She'll be all right.'

Her arms were throbbing from their gripping hands. Her face was wet with tears that she hadn't noticed pouring from her eyes. There was a crack of light now on the horizon, red like flames. The corporal gave her a gentle push in the direction of the line. She started to walk. His footsteps followed her. She stopped.

'What are they going to do with him?'

The engines cut out and the boat drifted towards the shore.

'Get on, Miss. Do get on.'

She was bitterly cold. She moved on again towards the blocks. Climbing up over the granite. Up on the line she looked back. Two soldiers were hoisting the body into the boat. The earth was colouring now. There would be no traces soon.

'Miss, I haven't all day, you know.'

She nodded and they walked along the line.

'What will they do with him?' she asked the question quietly.

'Dispose of him,' was all the answer she got. After that they walked in silence.

At the gate she turned to him.

'I go up here. It's all right. You can leave me now.'

He looked doubtfully at her.

'I promise. I'll just go straight home.'

'I dunno . . .'

'You see, you'll upset my aunt dreadfully if you wake her up and start telling her all this. Please.'

'Orders, Miss.'

'I promise. My Grandfather's a general . . . well, a retired general.'

'All right. You get on home to bed. And don't you go round blabbing or you'll be in real trouble.'

'I'd really like to know why they did that.'

'They must have their reasons.'

A bird twittered uneasily above them from its nest.

'They make the decisions, we do what we're told. That's the way of life.'

'I don't think he saw it like that.'

'That's why they wanted him dead. There's your answer. Go home now, Miss, and keep your face shut.'

He turned and walked away.

The house was still and peaceful.

She looked at her face in the glass on her dressing table. Her eyes were swollen with tears and shock. She dropped her clothes on the floor and fell naked on to her bed. The light from the growing sun was widening across the ceiling. Red sky in the morning. I will never be able to sleep again. The swallows scratched in the eaves. Sleep or laugh or love or swim in the sea which is now filled with his blood. Be happy, never be happy. The great illusion. We all seek for an illusion. That's all. I will never again . . . never . . . I . . . She slept.

She awoke the next morning as usual to the sound of Aunt Mary's bath water running down the pipes. Golly, I must get up, she thought, and then remembered what had happened in the night! Or perhaps it had been a nightmare? If she went down to the hut, he would still be there, sitting with his back to the wall reading. Had he, in fact, existed? There would be no trace of him. No blood on the sand. No footmarks. No spent bullets. It was Sunday. The bells would ring in the two churches in the village. The only thing to do is to get up. She sat up and swung her legs over the side of the bed. Her second toe was still longer than her first one. Nothing had changed. There was sand on the floor. Bridie would have a word or two to say about that. Oh dear God, let him have peace now! He didn't get his bottle of claret. I feel so heavy, full of shame and sadness. Sunday clothes. Spit and polish.

There were no papers on Sunday, so Aunt Mary was reading a book when Nancy went into the dining room.

'Good morning, dear. I hope you slept well.'

Nancy kissed her aunt.

'Umm!'

'I didn't, I must say. I couldn't stop thinking of that awfulness yesterday. Pour out your own coffee, dear, I've got sticky fingers. I suppose there'll be reprisals now. No one can ever leave anything alone. We'll walk to church today, dear. I feel the need to clear my head.'

'It's going to rain.'

'A little rain won't hurt us. It may hold off until after lunch.'

'Sun before seven, rain before eleven.' It was just something to say.

'I wonder if they found the man they were looking for.

156

I do hope it isn't poor Angoose.'

'Hmm!'

'Harry and Maeve are coming to lunch. I hope you'll behave terribly well.'

'I will. Honestly.'

'That's good, dear. In a way I hope they don't find him. I'd hate to think of anything terrible hapening to him.' She shut her book. 'It really hasn't been a very happy few days.'

'No.'

'I rather suspect that Harry and Maeve are going to get engaged. Will that upset you?'

Nancy thought about it.

'No. Not a bit. Isn't that funny!'

'That's all right then. I wouldn't like you to be upset.'

She got up and looked around the room vaguely.

'We'll have to decide what we're going to sell and what we're going to keep.'

'I suppose so.'

'One becomes so attached to things.'

'Yes.'

'It'll be an adventure. New ground.'

'Yes.'

'Next week we must positively start to get organized.'

'Yes.'

'I must go and see to Father.'

She moved to the door.

'I think we'll have champagne for lunch. Wouldn't that be a good idea?'

'Yes.'

'And you'll be good?'

'I told you.'

'Give Bridie a hand to clear the table, there's a good girl.'

'Yes.'

As she opened the door and went out, the sound of the old scratchy voice came down the passage.

'I fear no foe with Thee at hand to bless, Ills have no weight and tears no bitterness . . .'

Nancy picked up the tray from the sideboard and began to pile it with plates. I ought to cry, but I can't. Anger and pain.

157

'Where is death's sting? Where grave thy victory?'

The door down the passage closed and the voice was lost.

The great thing is you can always choose, and then, as Bridie says, you've no one to blame but yourself.

Jennifer Johnston

HOW MANY MILES TO BABYLON?   1.50

THE CAPTAINS AND THE KINGS   £1.50

THE GATES   £1.50

THE CHRISTMAS TREE   £1.50

FONTANA PAPERBACKS

FLAMINGO

Flamingo is a quality imprint publishing both fiction and non-fiction. Below are some recent titles.

Fiction
- ☐ Separate Tracks *Jane Rogers* £2.50
- ☐ A Dry White Season *André Brink* £2.50
- ☐ Goosefoot *Patrick McGinley* £2.50
- ☐ Memed, My Hawk *Yashar Kemal* £2.95
- ☐ She Came to Stay *Simone de Beauvoir* £2.95
- ☐ The Woman Destroyed *Simone de Beauvoir* £1.95
- ☐ The Once and Future King *T.H. White* £3.95

Non-fiction
- ☐ A Book of Five Rings *Miyamoto Musashi* £1.95
- ☐ The Common People: a History from the Norman Conquest to the Present *J.F.C. Harrison* £3.95
- ☐ The Walled Kingdom: a History of China from 2000BC to the Present *Witold Rodzinski* £3.95
- ☐ Orwell *Raymond Williams* £1.95
- ☐ The Dancing Wu Li Masters *Gary Zukav* £2.95
- ☐ Hitler: The Führer and the People *J.P. Stern* £2.50
- ☐ Language Made Plain *Anthony Burgess* £2.50

You can buy Flamingo paperbacks at your local bookshop or newsagent. Or you can order them from Fontana Paperbacks, Cash Sales Department, Box 29, Douglas, Isle of Man. Please send a cheque, postal or money order (not currency) worth the purchase price plus 15p per book (maximum postal charge £3.00).

NAME (Block letters) _____

ADDRESS _____

_____

_____